DONALD SMITH was born in Glas[...] in Glasgow and Stirling, he beg[...] stage manager, becoming Direc[...] in 1983. Donald has written, dir[...] and is a founding Director of the National Theatre of Scotland.

Influenced by Hamish Henderson, Donald was also the moving spirit behind the new Scottish Storytelling Centre of which he is the first Director. One of Scotland's leading storytellers, he has produced a series of books on Scottish narrative, including *Storytelling Scotland: A Nation in Narrative, Celtic Travellers,* and a poetry collection, *A Long Stride Shortens the Road: Poems of Scotland.* *The English Spy,* his first novel, is set in the closes, courts and wynds of Edinburgh, the first UNESCO City of Literature.

Donald Smith's study of Robert Burns and religion *God, the Poet and the Devil,* is also published this year, the 250th anniversary of the birth of Burns.

Between Ourselves

DONALD SMITH

Luath Press Limited

EDINBURGH

www.luath.co.uk

First published 2009

ISBN (10): 1-906307-92-X
ISBN (13): 978-1-906307-92-9

The publisher acknowledges subsidy from

Scottish
Arts Council

towards the publication of this book.

The paper used in this book is recyclable. It is elemental chlorine free
(EFC) and manufactured from sustainable wood pulp forests. This
paper and its manufacture are approved by the National Association of
Paper Merchants (NAPM), working towards a more sustainable future.

Printed and bound by
Thomson Litho, East Kilbride.

Typeset in 11 point Sabon

To Edinburgh, in darkness and in light

What an antithetical mind! – tenderness, roughness – delicacy,
coarseness – sentiment, sensuality – soaring and grovelling – dirt and
deity – all mixed up in that one compound of inspired clay!
George Gordon, Lord Byron, on reading some 'unpublished and
never to be published' letters of Robert Burns

I paint the way some people write their autobiography. The paintings,
finished or not, are the pages of my journal and, as such, they are
valid. The future will choose the pages it prefers. It's not up to me to
make the choice.
Pablo Picasso, quoted by Françoise Gilat

One song of Burns is worth more to you than all I could think of for
a whole year in his native country. His misery is a dead weight on the
nimbleness of one's pen... he talked with Bitches... he drank with
Blackguards, he was miserable. We can see horribly clear in the works
of such a Man his whole life, as if we were God's spies.
John Keats

Author's Preface

WE KNOW A lot about Robert Burns. But who was he behind the masks, the depressions and the verbal fireworks?

A lot of people, including several who feature as characters in this novel, burned their correspondence from the poet, even demanding back their own letters after his death. The closer you were the more likely you were to destroy the evidence. We know that Agnes McLehose – the much misrepresented 'Clarinda' – doctored her intimate communications with 'Sylvander'. Burns' brother Gilbert was very tight-lipped when the first official biographer Dr Currie came calling. Already the mythology of Scotland's national poet was taking hold – a flawed icon but an icon nonetheless.

I have taken one intense period of Burns' life – six months in Edinburgh – as the focus of my story. Day by day, these months became the defining pivot between the Ayrshire years and the short-lived maturity in Dumfries. There is nothing here that contradicts the researchers, yet for a novelist there are significant and creative gaps. What was the balance of the relationships with Peggy Chalmers and Jean Armour, with Clarinda and Jenny Clow? Were there others? And who did Burns fraternise with in the city's lowlife haunts apart from his bosom cronies William Smellie and Bob Ainslie?

The women are at the heart of Burns' Edinburgh crisis. Why has Agnes McLehose been variously labelled flirt and prude, Calvinist and cocktease? What lay behind Jenny's stubborn refusal to give up her son to his father, even on her deathbed? I cannot pretend to fully recover these lost voices, but I have tried to listen to their accents and draw out their underlying experiences.

The reader also becomes party to these private communications. How do we tell the story of our own lives – selectively, confidingly, misleadingly? There are letters or emails, social masks and conventions. I am not making any judgements, least of all about Robert Burns, but I would like you to be on the inside of these relationships. In the end we all have to decide for ourselves.

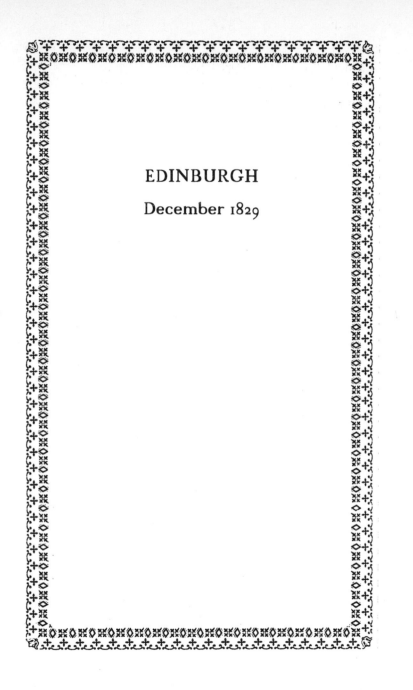

EDINBURGH

December 1829

Sarah was straining at the door to catch even a fragment of the conversation inside. But the voices were murmuring confidentially. The mistress received plenty of respectable callers, but a visit from Jean Armour, the widow of Robert Burns, was out of the ordinary, especially given the circumstances…

The sturdy old lady had arrived out of breath after walking all the way from the Glasgow coach stop in the Grassmarket. It was more than an hour since Sarah had taken in the tea, and been dismissed without pouring. Jean Armour was still a handsome figure, if a little stout.

In the cosy parlour discussion was drawing to a close.

'He wis guid-hearted in his ain nature, hoosoever he driftit times intae foolishness.'

'I believe that also. Robert's virtues will outshine his faults as long as he has true friends to defend him.'

'Aye an folk play fair.'

'Precisely.'

'Sae we're agreed. There's things aboot Rab naebody else need ken.'

'Apart from us.' Nancy's eyes moved from the brown paper package between them to the wine glasses on the dresser which had been Burns' last gift.

'It's been my wish since I turned up the box twa months syne. I culdna read it aa ower again. He wis bye wi it.'

'But you felt I had to be consulted.'

'That was it. Forbye we had never met. Is that no strange?'

Nancy leaned forward to put her dainty wrinkled hands on the countrywoman's knees, and looked into her eyes.

'You know, Jean, how much this still means to me.'

'Aye, I think ah dae. He's no easy forgotten.'

Nancy reached down and pushed forward the package.

Jean stood up heavily and lifted it onto the hearth. Stooping down she opened up the wrapping to reveal a scuffed journal bound in black leather and three bundles of manuscripts tied with faded ribbons.

For a moment they looked at the worn relics. Every inch seemed covered with writing. Bending again, Jean handed one bundle to Nancy and took one herself, and with a last glance at each other they sent the two bundles into the coals. Quickly flames began to lick round the edges, then the top pages curled, blazed and blackened. As the fire sprang to work Nancy threw on the last bundle and they watched it burn. Finally Jean had the journal in her strong hands. She opened it wide and tore out a handful of pages. In it went, than another and another until the end boards themselves lay on top of the bier.

Ten minutes later when Sarah finally opened the door unsummoned to collect the tea things, the two old ladies were sound asleep beside a dying fire. A brown paper wrapper was loose on the rug and a thick wadge of paper with singed edges lay on top of the smouldering coals.

EDINBURGH
October 1787
to New Year 1788

THE JOURNAL

LAST STAY IN Edinburgh but not for long; hardly worth the notice.

But this sheaf of paper begun so many months ago is an accumulation of empty sheets, a harvest of nothings. I intended the observation of men and manners, reflection and self-knowledge, fields of science and some sheltered glades of poetry. Now the days and weeks stare back at me like featureless faces.

What is it about this place that gnaws the guts and nips my head? Why at ease with Scotland and out of sorts in Edinburgh?

Even arriving with acclaim already in my pocket, I spent the first week on a straw pallet with a sour belly. A sore mind turned in on itself. Now I am here marking time. How to arrive in Edinburgh?

Notwithstanding, my lodgings have moved upwards. Then I shared a bed with Richmond, barely raised above the stinking High Street causeway. Carts carting, criers crying, pisspots pouring and floozies fleering. The land-lady demanded an extra eightpence since her mattress was burdened by two bodies in turn. What if it had been simultaneous?

Today I lord it in Newton, Edinburgh. My attic lair soars above St James Square, where the Old Town odours of gardez-loo are chased swiftly through gracious squares and out to sea by a stiff breeze. A sturdy timber bed, trig dresser with glass and two sash windows, one townward and one looking clear across to Fife. Auld Reikie is still in Scotland. This room might offer fresh perspective, given time and leisure.

Little Jean, the lassie of the house, comes tripping up to ask if I will take tea, and if I will hear her at the pianoforte. Both, of course, my lady, for neither can be refused. Nor should be. I must write a song for that sweet high voice. A song requites nature's promise to her bard.

To bed with a miserable cold. Head oozing, throat rasping, and that old familiar tightening. Will these tearing stounds of pain gripe me again? A hellish deathman swinging at my vitals with a rusty scythe. One drooking at the plough or an ill-considered journey can lay the honest farmer on his back, at the mercy of his tormentors.

My weakness brings Betty from the kitchen hearth with a mustard poultice, steaming infusions and soothing toddies. An old countrywoman normally cooped below decks, she ascends with bulging eyes and wagging chins like an officious turkey. Loosing my shirt and breeches, she kneads at chest and belly, strong fingers teasing out swellings and inflammation.

I surrender myself to firm handling. Easeful relief, then pleasure. As my mind empties I inhale these pungent odours and let the muscles breathe out. For a moment I am a babe again in Betty Davidson's sunburnt hands. Or a corpse to be anointed before wrapping in a shroud.

When I revived, Betty of St James Square had departed with all her cloths and steaming bowls.

Wrote a letter to Miller promising to come and see his farm as soon as I am better. Is this the offer which cannot be refused?

Much easier. But if I lie low Betty may climb again to minister to the poet, his body sliding back beneath snaw white linen. Birth, death and all the inbetweens rolled into one seamless consummation. Not today.

Comfortably on the pot for the first time in Edinburgh.

My desire for Peggy Chalmers is unlike anything I have felt before. With a mind as bright as her frame, Peggy is fresh and finely moulded. I want Peggy Chalmers who is my equal in every way. But she is denied me as if prison bars were fixed between us from head to foot. Without these she would rush into my arms. Our eyes spoke everything her tongue denied. And then she looked away.

It cannot be, her body cried. Why not? Why should the blind tyranny of social laws prevail? Are we not born to natural freedom? Or to harsh necessity. So I am banished back to books and rhymes, mocked by my first resolution on coming to the capital.

'I am determined to make these pages my confidante.' As well I might since no-one else attends my inmost feelings. Intimacy declined, the poet should consult his own entrails.

'I will sketch every character who catches my notice with unshrinking justice.' Some I can still bring to the bar; they know who they are. 'Likewise my own story, my amours, my rambles.'

Well, circulating libraries may be supplied – the smiles and frowns of fortune on my bardship. Scotia mother of my dreams, should we be shamed by what we are at birth?

'My poesy and fragments that never see the light of day will be inserted.' Last year's resolution. I could renew that pact, given sufficient leisure. Or is it boredom. Four shillings for the book with black endboards. So little can hardly have purchased so much friendship since confidences went to market. Honesty for sale! I'm in Edinburgh now, God help me. A glass of wine with soup may do no harm.

This is the drawing up of accounts. Then I can settle this business for once and all. I pull my chair up to the little table by the window.

The clouds are chasing each other over Calton Hill.

A package has arrived for me. A book, they say, passing it up by floors. A book for Mr Burns; its for the poet. The package sits in the centre of my table.

Pride of place, sirs, for *The Scots Musical Museum,* Volume One. Good old Jamie Johnson. A poor craftsman he may be but between these covers is the authentic spirit of Scotland. And two of my songs – 'Green Grow the Rashes' and 'Young Peggy Blooms my Bonniest Lass'. Not the last Peggy, I swear. And I found him a rounded version of 'Bonnie Dundee', both verses. Though I still twinge when patching lines and stanzas to mend the shattered wrecks of these venerable compositions.

Johnson, sir, I salute you. A glass please for Caledonia's true bard and only Muse – the People! Is there no brimming glass to hand? Aye, sneer if you care, drawing rooms of Edinburgh. A curse on your whinstane hearts, you Edinburgh gentry. But wait, who is that preening in the shadows? The Edinburgh Edition of Robert Burns. Stand aside and listen to Nature's Muse.

> Young Peggy blooms our bonniest lass
> Her blush is like the morning
> The rosy dawn, the Spring grass,
> With early gems adorning.

Pity I cannae sing, but needs must in the absence.

'It all began, your Ladyship, with old fragments found among our Peasantry in the west. Poor forgotten things, I had no idea anybody cared for them. I who had once known so many had forgotten them.'

Yes, indeed, heaven-taught ploughman.

'The Poetic Genius of my country found me as the prophetic bard Elijah did Elisha, at the plough – and threw her inspiring mantle over me. She bade me sing the loves, the joys, the rural scenes and pleasures of my natal soil in my native tongue. I tuned my wild artless notes as she instructed. And more—'

There is more?

'She whispered to me, come to the ancient metropolis of Caledonia, and lay your songs under my honoured protection. Now I obey her dictates and present to you, The Edinburgh Edition.'

And then she farted.

This is no time for petty reckonings. I must go and toast Johnson. Let Creech and his Edition wait tomorrow. Unhand me, Betty. The poet is whole again in all his parts.

Word is out; the poet is back. One brief sojourn at Dowie's and Mr Burns' public begins to clamour for further appearances. Prepare to repel boarders. The lumbering apeman Smellie and sleek man-about-town Bob Ainslie will have at us.

We form a trinity of sword, pen and pintle.

As for my printer, the reckoning is nigh.

Monies owed by William Creech bookseller to Robert Burns, Poet, for the Edinburgh Edition of his *Works*:

500 subscription copies £125
Balance Owing for Distribution to Subscribers £400
Property of Poems £100

Damn the bookseller's discount. Restate as—

Subscription copies £125.00
Subscribers' copies
(less discount at one quarter) £300.00
Property of Poems £105.00

£530.00

A tidy addition all of which Mr Creech has under his capacious belt, tightly fastened. More Leech than Creech. First call today.

Must also draft and deliver notes for Johnson. Volume One demands its successor like a lusty child brothers and sisters. Let us deliver the new arrivals to Scotland's glory.

Interleaved notes in draft for James Johnson

One. Set lines to tunes nearer than printed.
Two. To 'Here Awa, There Awa' must be added this, the best verse in the song:

Gin ye meet my love, kiss her an clap her,
An gin ye meet my love, dinna think shame:
Gin ye meet my love, kiss her an clap her,
An show her the way to haud awa hame.
There's room on the printer's plate.

Three. For the tune of the Scotch queen, take the two first and the two last stanzas of 'The Lament' in Burns' Poems.

Four. 'To Daunton Me' – the chorus is set to the first part of the tune, which just suits it when played or sung over once. So to set:

The blude red rose at Yule may blaw,
The summer lilies bloom in snaw,
The frost may freeze the deepest sea
But an auld man shall never daunton me
To daunton me, to daunton me
An old man shall never daunton me.

And auld Creech shall never daunton me. Let the piper be paid for his tunes. But for Jamie the lark, the throstle and the doo shall sound their woodnotes wild without restraint or hindrance.

Blue devils.
Ainslie put off for tonight. He may call in.

Interleaved page of letter to James Hay, Librarian and Composer to the Duke of Gordon

Allow me, Sir, to strengthen the small claim I have to acquaintance by the following request.
An Engraver, James Johnson in Edinburgh has, not from mercenary views but from an honest Scotch enthusiasm, set about collecting all our native songs and setting them to music; particularly those that have never been set before. Clarke, the well known musician, presides over the musical arrangement; and Drs Beattie and Blacklock, Mr Tytler of Woodhouslee, and your humble servant to the utmost of

his power, assist in collecting the old poetry, or sometimes to make a stanza or a fine air when it has no words.

My request is 'Cauld Kail in Aberdeen', intended for this number, and I beg a copy of His Grace of Gordon's words to it, which you were so kind as to repeat to me. You may be sure we won't prefix the Author's name, except you like. Though I look on it as no small merit that the names of many of the Authors of our old Scotch Songs will be inserted in this work. Johnson's terms are for each Number, a handsome pocket volume, to consist of at least a hundred songs, with basses for the Harpsichord etc; the price to subscribers five, and to non subs six shillings. I rather write at you, but if you will be so obliging as on receipt of this to write me a few lines.

Damn all prevarications, but most of all their supreme commander, William Creech.

Harmoniously pissing and shitting as never before in Auld Reikie. On all other fronts ceasefire prevails.

She has a serious face beneath those tightly formed ringlets. The hair sits close round a finely moulded head. But she holds her head forward, shyly almost, above the slender neck. Hazel eyes, soulful; a strong nose (too strong?); the firm rosebud of a mouth; distant chin; breasts clear and pointed despite her diffident stance.

She listens intensely, submissive on the surface, then when she moves or speaks everything is alive, alight in motion. The eyes dance with flecks of understanding, a gleam of mischief.

My Peggy's face, my Peggy's form
The frost of hermit age might warm.
My Peggy's worth, my Peggy's mind
Might charm the first of humankind.

I love my Peggy's angel air
Her face so truly heavenly fair
Her native grace so void of art
But I adore my Peggy's heart.

Climbing ahead of me on the slope to Castle Campbell. She weaves nimbly through the trees, small but sure, perfectly poised. She turns to laugh at me clambering behind, her head haloed through sunlit leaves. What could I not be with such a soulmate, a polestar, a guide, a dancing delight? She brings out the best in me. I don't boast to Peggy but share only my honest satisfactions. Like Mr Skinner's poem in my praise – she knows its worth. I tell her the sensible things she wants to hear. On Thursday I will go to inspect Mr Miller's farm – like the honest tiller of the soil she has in mind. My own Minerva. But she will not have me.

I used every resource of elegance – flourishes of hand, heart melting meditations, modulations of winning speech. All vain. My rhetoric's usual effect is lost on her at least. She puts my sincerity to quiet scorn.

When did that arise? Why?

Peggy Chalmers stood apart; she held out against me. When she stayed on her father's farm in Mauchline, I used to visit. Hers was a family lowered from high estate, yet connected to the best society. I passed smoothly from formal bows – the awestruck swain – to a careless arm around the waist. She brought me up hard and short, laying out in no uncertain terms the distance I had still to travel.

Yet I kept my head, cool and deliberate under fire. I asked her to forgive poor Rab o Mossgiel, whose only fault, whatever rank he had in life, was in loving her too much for his own peace. I had no formal design, outwith the nakedness of my own heart in this matter-of-fact tale. Of course she might wish to cut me off, imposing in effect a complete cure for lovestruck rustics. Or she might allow me to renew the beaten path of friendship.

That brought her back into line and when we met again in Edinburgh my devotions were a morning walk, heartfelt conversation, books and poetry, now and then a glance or pressure of the hand. Rarely, in some sequestered spot, I chance a gentle touch of lip on cheek, lip on lip.

Might Caledonia's Bard not now aspire to Peggy's lifelong companionship, crowning Miss Chalmers' sweet company?

She teased me about my French and then paired me with a French lady who had no English, to catch me out. I failed miserably but she translated smoothing out my *faux pas*. Minerva of the school bench, sweet Sophia.

Peggy's song must go into Johnson's next volume along with 'The Lofty Ochils', recalling those precious days at Harvieston. I have set it to Neil Gow's 'Lament for Abercairny', proving my devotion. Her cousin Charlotte's song belongs there too along with the air I got at Inverness.

> How pleasant the banks of the clear-winding Devon
> With green-spreading bushes, and flowers blooming fair
> But the bonniest flower on the banks of the Devon

Was once a sweet bird on the braes of the Ayr.

All it needs is a fiddle and a Neil Gow.

Then back to Mauchline I went to the prying tongues. No more sunlit raptures or twilight *tête-à-têtes* beneath the shady hills. Just restless cares not knowing which way to turn. Farming is the only thing I know, and little enough at that, but it's a life that killed my father. Now they threaten to break up what remains of my closest family.

I could not settle to my mind. Should I try again for Jamaica? To stay at home without fixed aim would only dissipate my gains from the Kilmarnock poems, and ruin what compensation I could leave my little ones for the stigma I brought on them. The welcome weans.

Yet I did have my Mauchline belle, my Juno. After the poetic jaunts she pulled me back to herself. What a relief to spend my pent up emotion into her moist warmth. For weeks and months I had been starved, straining at polite intercourse. Sometimes in Edinburgh I went down from Dowie's tavern in the darkness and had some Cowgate wench, skirts lifted, hard against the wall, for a few coppers. But Jean's lovemaking was full and open as the hills of Ayrshire, an honest passion, a body made to be caressed and yoked. Often I took her working breasts into my mouth till nippled hard and sunk my member into her passage. Soft belly under taut muscles rise and fall as boats on a swelling sea.

That was country love. Rab o Mossgiel in rut. Dear Jean's only reading is the Psalms of David, and of course a certain book of Scots poems to which she is devoted.

But Peggy Chalmers will not marry me. Why? She touches tenderly on my feelings, my friendship, my talents, even as she refuses me. But of her own feelings not one word. Her reasons for turning down the ploughman poet? Is she too high for lowly Burns? Her father farms like mine. Too refined for Rab o Mossgiel? We made one happy party beneath the Ochils, conversed as equals, discussed men and women, books and the lovely world. These are the happiest days I have ever known. By Minerva's native glades and streams. Have I no reason left to hope? What's wrong with Robert Burns?

She will surely like these songs, the declaration of a poet's love. And old Tullochgorum's paid the highest tribute to my Muse. I must copy Mr Skinner's letter for her. I value his praise more highly than the approbation or disdain of a roomful of Edinburgh's literati. He too has drunk at the mountain springs of auld Scotia's Muse. There is a certain something in the older Scotch songs, a wild aptness of thought and expression, which marks them out not only from English songs but from the modern efforts of our native song wrights. We sons of Caledonian song must hang thegither and challenge the jury of fashion. We can lash that world and find ourselves an independent happiness.

I wonder if they have begun to talk about Jean's appearance in Mauchline.

With Bob Ainslie and Willie. Came home later.

I have seen Mr Miller's two farms lying prettily by the Nith. Both are up for lease but the ground is sour and the house at Ellisland half fallen down. O for a Horace in the desert wastes.

Passable evening despite my troubles.

After a drink in Anchor Close we went on to Dowie's. Very private and snug. Smellie was full of some pamphlets from America, newly bound for discreet sale. Some are by Tom Paine, an English Exciseman before going to the Colonies to champion the cause of liberty. By Willie's lights, Paine has demolished monarchy, for if the power of kings had to be checked by parliaments, how could it be ordained of God? Despotic rule is therefore contrary to natural justice and divine law.

Yet parliament itself in London defers to hereditary principle with benchfuls of m'lords sitting in judgement on the people's representatives, such as they are. A member of parliament may be elected by thirty comfortably dined men. The purpose of government, says Paine, is to preserve liberty and restrain the will of rulers. Where then the ancient King of Scots? Were they not defenders of our nation's freedoms? Is government now not tyranny by another name?

The natural right of men, and women – here Smellie raised a romantic glass which we were compelled to follow – is to be free and to have that freedom protected by representation. I believe this from my heart yet my head is overtaken in the race. Where America has gone will Britain follow, or France, or Spain? Bob was very douce. Does he class Smellie's lectures as philosophy or as sedition? He keeps his own counsel.

Ainslie has no political passion, no inner fire for freedom. The lawyer's clerk sits perjink, sleekit even, in the courts and taverns. Yet in his mind every mischief buzzes like a byke of hungry bees. No thought too low for Bob to comprehend, no slight so trivial that it escapes the tally. His ever listening ear sips up my nonsense with a sympathetic snigger. Wayward fancies pile one upon another till the crazy tower comes tumbling down. But if blue devils rise, Bob is my perpetual ally, sure defence and sole protection.

It was Ainslie, a few nights since, that whispered Hastie's Close into my ear. There he claimed gambling, cockfights and other bodily combats were to be had for easy money. Entry should to be petitioned and obeisance made to a Prince of those infernal regions. Don't ask who, Bob croaked, a warning finger pressed to his pouting lips.

The other two had drunk over deeply to go anywhere except home. But my incapacity for wine left me strangely lucid, light-headed on a cold and starry night. In their stupor Bob and Willie presumed that I was after Cowgate warmth, so I took the narrow passage down, crossed into Hastie's Close and tapped at the forementioned door. My assurance gained admission to the fringes of a scene of fervour such as Mauchline scarcely boasts. The Prince seemed absent and I escaped unscathed. Bob will want to weasel out the tale, but I can guard this secret for myself perhaps to go again in some idle hour.

No word from Creech. Peggy's letter expected daily.

Refused. Publication outlawed.

None outside her circle would know and those who do admit the justice of my praise. Poetic compliments cannot be misinterpreted. Moreover what I sketched are mental charms without a hint of impropriety. Away with sheepish modesty, my lovely Peggy Chalmers. Besides both pieces are set to music and ready at the printer's desk. To be blunt, woman, your looks are somewhat above the mean, but it's your wit that justifies my verse. I must get out my pen and persuade her that Caledonia's Bard cannot hurt her. Or else change the names. These are not the japes of Rhymer Rab – is that what she thinks of me?

Life is too short for these jarring passages. In a week I should be in Ayrshire, then on for Nithside. I cannot wait in Edinburgh on a lady's whim and pleasure.

Her letter to the young heir is apt though. She sends me it in confidence knowing she can depend upon my discretion. In sober moments the young fool admits his selfishness. Given his unsteadiness, the circumstances in which he finds himself, his father's disposition and a thousand other not-to-be-disregarded niceties, the whole affair with Charlotte is fantastic. Peggy's letter brings him down to earth though not severely, and he did not take it amiss. It's me she denies outright. Still the young idiot insists on gratifying inclination at the enormous and cruel expense of Charlotte's peace – the very woman for whom he professes undying love. A volatile schoolboy who knows two times two better than a woman's heart. *Tant pis*. May the Devil take all these brats before the amiable and lovely go down under their purse-proud contempt.

Can Peggy not see my position in all this? Her natural ally and judicious friend, a spiritual helpmate and comforter. What's the point? My time is nearly done with Edinburgh and genteel society. The hour has run – tomorrow will decide my affairs with Creech.

'Mr Burns, good day to you, sir, and welcome. No, the pleasure is all mine.' And before I can take up my point, 'Come through now, there is company already gathered.'

'Mr Creech, I need to… I would be very grateful if you might see—'

'We have Mr Fergusson here today and our distinguished editor, your good friend, Mr Smellie...' All the while gently patting and ushering me through to the main shop, where Edinburgh's literati minor and major are assembled.

'I need to settle my affairs.' Turned like a stubborn sheep in the gate.

'Come now, Mr Burns, it is too early for gentlemen to settle business. All will be attended to later.'

'You are already very behindhand, Mr Creech.'

'Ah you are a poet. Young authors must become accustomed to how things proceed in the world. Had Mr Smellie rushed *Encyclopaedia Britannica* in this way he would never have passed the first volume. Gracious, here is one of our learned divines, Reverend Kemp of the Tolbooth. Have you sat under him? Mr Kemp! How can I be of assistance today?'

The poet creeps away to join in general conversation...

Went on with Smellie to Anchor Close and drank to the damnation of all printers. Later in the afternoon, Creech himself came in all affability, discoursing widely on the decline of morals 'in our fair town.' 'Why,' says he, 'at one time Sunday was strictly observed as a day of devotion but now people stroll about at all hours, and the evenings are often loose and riotous with bands of young apprentices.' He seemed to eye me at this stage as if to say, 'and young poets.' 'The fines for bastard children have risen fivefold in the last ten years.' I put my money on the table and left.

Johnson much dispirited. Sales of *The Museum* have barely met expenses and he despairs of a second volume. I encouraged his honest soul. Perhaps this is not a profitable endeavour, but it will endure. You, sir, are a patriot for the music of your country, and we know how Scotland rewards patriots. But if we proceed steadily and correctly your name will be immortal. In the long run the textbook and standard of Scottish song will have a long-lasting sale, if maybe not a huge market. He seemed comforted. I took some soup with Mrs Johnson and teased the bairns. What a genuine, good-hearted fellow he is; I will do everything in my power to aid him.

Expenses are mounting with no with no relief from Creech. How long can I afford to wait? Yet what hope is there of securing payment if I leave?

Miller is a gentleman but his latest letter hints clearly at the need for a decision on this damned farm.

The ever plausible Creech cannot deny my dues. There it is in Mackenzie's own venerable hand – six hundred pounds at least, less bookseller's accursed discount. How long can he hold out against me? I cannot eat further into the Kilmarnock money.

Hard gripes again today roun my heart. Is it fear, the spectre of haggard poverty, who preys on the poor and wastes their flesh?

Jean is waiting for me in Mauchline. I made her no promises – the ones I did make were torn up in my face. Now Armour would almost pay me to wed his daughter.

No courage to go out. Betty brought me up a dish of stew. She has a tender spot for the will o the wisp poet.

Glanced idly at some songs that will help Johnson's second volume.

Ainslie, Smellie, with myself, Beugo the engraver, Nasmith and Captain Henderson (both neighbours here in James' Square) made a merry party. Simple food married with good music. When we finished the night was young, so I sampled Hastie's Close again with more substantial satisfactions.

Beugo is doing my phiz. It can appear in future looking like all other fools on my title page. I will be as famous as John Bunyan or Blind Milton, and have my poor birthday in the almanac along with Black Monday and the Battle of Bothwell Brig.

Let them adorn the editions, for there will not be many more additions. My familiar Muse seems to have abandoned me, chafed and wearied by the little fat gods of criticism. My recent poetry has been tried before an Edinburgh jury and found wanting. My verse is condemned as a libel against the fastidious ranks of taste. My satires are deemed defamation, the author forbidden to print on pain of – of what? Forfeiture of character, of reputation. Of the means of livelihood. There they have me. I cannot supplicate the Muses empty handed.

I should have stayed plain Rhymer Rab and strung my woodnotes wild for those who recognised and understood them. Let those who have lugs hear.

It was Gavin Hamilton's idea to print, and that led to Kilmarnock. Friend and landlord, he defended me against the godly crew, for he had his own quarrel with Holy Willie. So the gentlemen of Ayrshire subscribed, as well as ministers, farmers, and all the brothers of the lodge. Without their guineas I would have gone to Jamaica, but their notice secured Henry Mackenzie's praise. His was the Mason's word that hailed the heaven-taught ploughman and secured my entry to Edinburgh, a new Man of Feeling.

Instead of taking ship I was borne on a tide of acclamation. Yet Kilmarnock brought no end to servitude; it was but the prelude to greater obligation. With each new mark of favour dependence on my patrons grows. Letters, visits and dedications pile higher than the poems which they profess to honour.

'Fate has cast my station in the veriest shades of life, but never did a heart pant more ardently than mine to be distinguished.'

'How supremely I was gratified in being honoured with the countenance and approbation of one of my dear loved country's most illustrious sons.'

'Allow me, my Lord, to proffer my warm and fond request to be permitted to publish these verses.'

'So, my Lord, I must return to my rustic station and in my wonted way woo my rustic Muse at the plough stand. Still, my Lord, while the drops of life, while the sounds of Caledonia warm my heart, gratitude to that dear-prized country in which I boast my birth, and gratitude to those her distinguished names who have honoured me so much with their approbations and patronage, shall, while stealing through her humble shades, ever distend my bosom and at times draw forth the swelling tear... like pustules fit to burst.'

'I have the honour to be with the highest respect, your much indebted humble servant, Robert Burns,' you windy old arse-ship, who likes 'these little Doric pieces of yours in our provincial dialect' and tells me to keep my eye on Parnassus 'while warding off the pleasures of wine'.

Yet I owe the Edinburgh Edition entirely to the Earl

of Glencairn, Dalrymple of Orangefield, Dean Erskine of Faculty, and the young bucks of the Caledonian Hunt. Now suddenly in Mauchline they doff their bonnets to Rab, as if he were some revelation of new birth, regenerate flesh, an heir to high estate, instead of plain Burns. Even James Armour, who tried to tear the coat off my back, crawls up to mouth inane servilities. His slimy tongue pollutes Jean's honest image in my mind. I should have spat in his face.

Why should I doff my cap again and settle for a country lass, when I can woo the true-born Muse? The simpering drawing rooms boast no Muse except gentility and servitude. Edinburgh wants all its singers castrati.

I have a good song in hand for Johnson. It's the speech of James MacPherson below the gallows. Fiddler and half gypsy, he defied the world at the last and broke his beloved fiddle over the knee. 'No other hand will play on your strings when I am dead and gone.' And every woman in the crowd felt his caress.

All my reading now is in Milton's scripture. The sentiments, the dauntless magnanimity, the intrepid unyielding independence, the daring and noble defiance of that great hero, Satan, in the face of adversity.

A fig for those by law protected!
Liberty's a glorious feast!
Courts for Cowards were erected,
Churches built to please the Priest.

His book is always in my pocket.

At the Lodge in springtime, the Grand Master with all the Grand Lodge of Scotland visited. A numerous and elegant gathering of all the lodges about town. The

Grand Master presided with great solemnity, and among his general toasts he gave, 'Caledonia and Caledonia's Bard, Brother Burns!' It ran through the whole assembly and I sat dumb, thunderstruck. But truly that is all I now desire – the appellation of a Scottish bard, and to continue to deserve it. Scottish themes and Scottish notes are my *basso profundo*. If only I could sound them unplagued by business, for which, heaven knows, I am unfit.

At Ochertyre John Ramsay had a copse of willows planted round a carved inscription: 'To live in peace and die in joyful hope, within this small but pleasant inheritance of his fathers.' A Scots Horace retires from the din and dissipation to his pleasing sufficiency, leisure for intellectual pursuits pursued with steady discrimination. Independence of soul and loyal devotion to the Muse, undergirded with some modest rentals.

Would Miller's Ellisland give me exercise of mind and body with freedom of the spirit? I have already strained my mortal frame to breaking at the plough, drudging labour bound to the unyielding dirt. Was Ramsay or Horace ever harnessed to the ox?

Nasmith's portrait of me is a true likeness, neither rough nor smooth. He has given it without fee for my engraving. The tribute of friendship to my Muse. He and I watched the dawn rise over Rosslyn together, while the Esk flowed on through its wooded glens. I must not disfigure or deface such a homage.

Creech insists on a glossary of Scotch words and phrases for the next impression – to aid those unfamiliar with our homely speech. Aye and apologise for our own language and national literature. Did Douglas add a glossary when he translated Virgil's Latin? Did Allan Ramsay hedge *The Gentle Shepherd* with a bairns' primer? This is the Edinburgh fashion to eschew our native speech and erase 'Scotticisms of the tongue'. He has his eye on sales in London and in America.

Two-faced, double-tongued town, you have your perfect mouthpiece, your sublime orifice in William Creech.

You eunuch of language who gelds the poets pith, you Englishman who never ventured south of Tweed, you quack of elocution, you Gretna Green of vowels and consonants, you blacksmith hammering the rivets of absurdity, you butcher of orthographic disembowelling, you pitch-pipe of affected emphasis, you pimp of gender, you Lyon Herald to silly etymology, you executioner of grammar, you scape-gallows from the land of syntax, you scavenger, you pickle herring in the puppet-show of nonsense, you recording angel of barbarous idiom, you baleful meteor foretelling and facilitating the descent to Erebean night. Sleep well, for tomorrow is our day of reckoning.

A miserable dank haar has crept up, enveloping all the chimney steeps of Auld Reikie. A day to sit by the fire and brood. As the chill steals in our windows, a hot toddy supplements the best effort of Newcastle coals.

Now I can tell what I saw in Hastie's Close. For your eyes only, my trusty confidante.

As before, a light knock gained admittance to the outer chambers. There, the keepers – messengers, attendants – sat slumped around two or three tables dimly lit by tallow lamps, awaiting events.

This antechamber is also a gateway or crossroads since from there you can see further chambers and passages opening in every direction. Move right or left, up or down, and you slip deeper into a torch lit warren.

Below, a tight-packed array of tables marks the gamblers' den. At two crowded boards, dice rattle. At another, kings, queens and jacks are ranked against each other. And on all sides, the same assembling of stakes, piles of glinting coins, cries of despair, hands slapped down in triumph. Girls of the town serve porter, wine and whisky, receiving leers, taunts and rough handling as their due.

Up ahead, you enter a different kingdom. The rooms are swathed in damask hangings and Turkish rugs. Coarseness is subdued by a presiding madam, arrayed like the hostess of an aristocratic drawing room, but more richly. Callers are ushered onto cushioned settles and soothed with wine. From an inner recess, women enter one by one for selection and delight, leading their purchasers back into a honeycomb of little rooms beyond. I watched with fascination, like a traveller to an Oriental palace, but declined, preferring to take my exercise *en plein air*.

Back to the antechamber. The right turn narrows onto a steep, wooden stair. Down it goes in three deep stages, far below the Cowgate. Darkness closes around the stale airs until at the lowest rung a blaze of torches bursts on the eye. A ring of faces, black mouths hanging open, presses forward, flickering in a sheen of eager lust. At the centre of the pack a whirl of hate, frenzied, goaded beyond bearing, torn and slashed by armoured spurs and sharpened beaks. For one brief moment all are held in violent consummation. Blood seeps into the filthy sand and one limp feathered creature lies inert. No notice paid as the mangled winner is scooped up and strident voices call wagers to set up the next cruel conflict.

I turn away, bile rising in my throat. How can man

out-beast nature and do the Devil's work without a devil's prompting? Breath clammy in my face, a vile mouth urges the superiority of dog fights, the promised climax of the night's proceedings. I clamber back up the steps, retching as I go. I want to break out into the cold night air, see starlight above the roofs. But in the antechamber an attendant catches my arm. The Deacon is asking to see me; will I step this way.

I am firmly steered into a room on the left. Two or three steps take me up into a formal rectangular space. A handsome, oval table first draws the eye, as the light is coming from a silver branched candelabra glowing on its polished surface. Around the candles, decanters and crystal goblets glint.

'Good evening, Mr Burns, you are very welcome.'

The voice is low in pitch, even in tenor, Scots, but measured and formal in the English style. As my vision adjusts I make out a compact figure at the other end of the table, an elegantly cut coat with brocaded waistcoat. The face is broad with deeply recessed eyes surmounted by arched brows. Their blackness is accentuated by a white powdered wig above.

'Please, join me for a glass of claret.'

He gestures towards a high-backed chair and takes another for himself. I notice a merchant's tricorn hat set to one side and, leaning against his chair, a knobbed cane.

'We had not anticipated the honour of a visit from our distinguished poet. I must apologise. Had we known, I would have arranged a guided tour.'

'Curiosity drew me,' I replied hesitantly.

'Naturally. It begins that way and then curiosity draws you back.'

He poured a full glass of mellow liquid for me and then

one for himself. 'I hope you like wine, Mr Burns. This is the best Bordeaux has to offer our Auld Alliance.'

I took a sip.

'Who are you, sir, if I may be bold to ask?'

'They call me the Deacon. Here I answer to that name and to no other.'

'The Deacon it is. The wine is very pleasing.'

'Indeed. Perhaps if we become better acquainted I will tell you something of my life.'

'You do not seek fame or reputation?'

'Alas, that would be my undoing.'

And so it petered out in an exchange of small talk, casual pleasantries, as if for all the world we were not sitting at the door of hell. He seemed to enjoy my nervous glances and diffident remarks, his keen attention missing nothing. Throughout, the Deacon remained immovably calm and gracious.

'May I offer you further entertainment for the night?'

I declined, pleading a weak constitution, and took a clumsy leave, thanking my host for his cordial reception. What other variety might be on offer? How did he know I was there, or who I was? I must be more discreet in future, if I go again. Certainly I would like to find out more about the Deacon. What threads bind him to the daylight world? Ainslie will know but I should not raise his suspicions.

A welcome interruption – invited for supper later by little Jean. A rosebud of unblemished innocence. Put away the journal.

Stupid most of the day and unfit for any other labours. The fog clung round us turning daylight into night. Joined the Cruikshanks for supper, savouring every moment of kindness and honest fellowship round a homely table. Thanking my Maker for his mercies to us his children.

Met Woods the player by arrangement at his favourite coffee house. The theatricals are in crisis since I left on my tours – playhouse riven and almost ruined. I found Woods voluble, verging on ecstatic. All more thrilling than the stage dramas.

It began with *Venice Preserved.* Jackson the Manager decided to cast my confidant Woods, his former leading man, as Pierre, and his new rising light James Fennell as Jassier. This even though Woods had been accustomed to Jassier and Fennell to Pierre. In truth Fennell would rather have taken Pierre and my friend to have retained Jassier, since both were already proved before the public. But Jackson maintained his right to cast in the public's best interest, insisting that if need be he would play his leading men on alternate nights until a clear preference emerged. Worst of both worlds?

As it happened, it was Mr Fennell as lead on the opening night. He was cried down in the theatre with shouts of 'the Manager', 'bring on Woods' and so forth. Anyway Jackson stood firm. Next letters arrived at the stage door threatening assault and worse on Fennell if he did not give way. Night after alternate night the performance was drowned in the pit.

Who were the instigators? Not friends of Woods – William's only desire is to see the company thrive. A darker Edinburgh tide was running. Fennell is an Eton and Cambridge man used to the best standing in English society. Coming to Edinburgh he presumed the same, calling in the best drawing rooms of the town. But horror – he is an actor! There lies his offence: to transgress, as Woods put it, the invisible yet immutable laws of rank.

Had he only consulted the poet. Actors are toasted on Edinburgh stages but tainted in the town, especially New Town. Fennell might be supreme as either Jassier or Pierre, but taboo-breakers must be driven out beyond the pale.

Still, Jackson stood manfully by his player. Then suddenly the ground shifted under him. Rumour was rife that in the heat of his nightly conflict Fennell had used an unbecoming expression. O woe thrice woe, did he 'bloody' or 'damn' in the teeth of bloody and damnable Edinburgh? The final blow was dealt with a letter sent to Jackson and signed by one hundred and sixty advocates or solicitors, headed by Erskine Dean of Faculty and Solicitor-General Dundas. The text as William related was brief but deadly.

'We are of the opinion that Mr Fennell's late deportment to the public, and your conduct as a Manager, require a very ample apology from both; and that if Mr Fennell refuses to make such an apology, you ought immediately to dismiss him; and we take this method of intimating to you, that if this opinion is not complied with by Wednesday evening neither we nor our families will hereafter frequent your theatre, except that from our high regard to Mrs Siddons, we shall postpone executing our resolution till her engagement expires.'

The *coup de grâce*. Thus Edinburgh is governed. What theatre could persist abandoned by the lawyers and lairds of North Britain? Fennell was withdrawn. Yet that same Wednesday, a faction rose up in the boxes demanding Fennell. Poor Jackson was blamed and forced to publish his bookings for the side boxes in the press, vehemently denying he had admitted any clandestine claque into any part of the house, either before the doors were opened or by other covert means.

Fortunately for Jackson and his company, the sublime Siddons, whose voice alone is worth a symphony of music, had been engaged for the whole summer, and she held the house, even though the poor Manager was compelled to bring a second leading man from London at short notice and ruinous expense. This was Jackson's penalty for offending certain Edinburgh gentlemen. Dictators of taste and conscience, they bestride our narrow stage like canting ministers their pulpits. Without their patronage no voice is heard, no picture viewed, no volume printed. Even the English are helpless before them. I have ploughed that bitter furrow on my own account. Must speak with Jackson about writing Scottish dramas.

Coming home, a cordial letter waited on my table. I knew the hand immediately; Peggy and Charlotte are the favourite resting places of my souls on the weary journey through this thorny wilderness. God knows, I am ill-fitted for the struggle. I glory in being a poet, I want to be thought wise, I would be generous, I wish to be rich. But at bottom I am left outcast like a ne'er do well player.

A wan sun without light or warmth. I feel that horrid hypochondria pervading every atom of my body, and my soul. Nerves in a damnable state. Let them go to hell – I'll fight it out.

Invitation arrived to take tea next week at Miss Nimmo's, and all in order to meet a young friend who admires my poetry. Some worthy, gushing female, no doubt plain to boot. My limb is flaccid from lack of exercise, or even incentive.

Dumfries again tomorrow. One last inspection will decide for a farm in that county, or its back to brother Gilbert at Mossgiel, and some neighbouring kail patch. A return to old haunts could drag me back into old habits. Must shake them off, and scour the filth of Edinburgh from my boots.

Another note from dear Miss Nimmo, very concerned. I shall not miss her tea party on my return, but I expect at the least a bevy of princesses.

Breathe the life of the land, even in its dooly season, and the Muse revives. Pleased with this tender wee thing for Johnson. Will add some mended stanzas for an old tune. Mixed with thoughts of Jean and the pleasant banks of the bonnie Doon.

> As I gaed doon the water-side
> There I met my shepherd-lad,
> He rowed me sweetly in his plaid,
> And he caad me his dearie.
> *Caa the yowes to the knowes,*
> *Caa them where the heather grows,*
> *Caa them where the burnie rowes,*
> *My bonnie dearie.*

> Will ye gang down the water-side
> And see the waves sae sweetly glide
> Beneath the hazels spreading wide,
> The moon it shines fu clearly.
> *Caa the yowes to the knows,*
> *Caa them where the heather grows,*
> *Caa them where the burnie rowes,*
> *My bonnie dearie.*

Miss Nimmo's acquaintance answers to Agnes McLehose. A Nancy by choice, almost a widow apparently, and brimming with life. Our eyes played ball and racquet across the tea cups. She wants me, Mrs McLehose that is, to take tea in her rooms at Potterrow. I must find out more – she has poetic inclinations.

Unable to get out of bed. Had to call for Betty's help to hobble into my chair. My kindly hosts sent for Wood the surgeon.Confined now to quarters till things mend, useless limb stretched before me. Even pissing awkward. My God, what a fool. Fergusson would turn it into a poem. The journey to Leith of Rob the Rhymer and how he came home with one leg. A comic upset to Odysseus, wayward peregrinations that topple pious Aeneas from his pedestal.

Ainslie, Willie and self hired a chaise for our jaunt to Leith. Spanking brown pony with supple flanks, so a brisk spin ensued beneath bright sunshine and clouds. Were we chasing them or they us? We passed two fisher lasses on the road got up in the shawls, full skirts and handsome bodices of their calling. Empty creels. I drew the coachman to a halt and invited the sea maidens aboard, but they were having none of the poet's vessel. Pity, Nature had made them for love. They laughed and waved us off.

By the shore we set up court in the Ship Inn. Rob and Smellie were in high form, and the company grew as merchantmen and carriers looked in on us. We were joined by some local ladies of the entertaining kind. Our coachman made up one of the party. Toasts and songs followed each other. Willie became entangled on both sides, so the poet was obliged to take one wing in hand. Food and more drink came on. Willie began to sink but then rose again like Neptune from the waves, locks uncombed, wild-thatched and staring. Does he never shave himself? The salt air induced hunger. Food and more drink were brought. O, the seagoing life.

Coming out late, darkness had already wrapped itself around the quay. Black mastheads were the only pointers. We piled into the coach, pushing our guide before us. Spirits threatened to fall as we trotted out of the port, so Willie proposed a singing competition. Each would better the other, verse by verse with a new stanza. I can only remember a couple.

BURNS:
Saw ye my Maggie
Saw ye my Maggie
Saw ye my Maggie
Comin ower the lea

SMELLIE:
My Maggie has a mark
Ye'll find it in the dark
It's in below her sark
A little aboon her knee

The next was Bob, or maybe the coachman – I cannot ascribe each author's rights precisely.

My Maggie has a treasure
A hidden mine o pleasure
I'll howk it at my leisure
It's alone for me

And so on. The pace picked up and soon we were rattling merrily for home verse by verse, with Willie beating a roaring tempo and me leaning back in the swaying coach like an emperor returning in his triumphal chariot. It called to mind my own wild horse race on Lomondside, when a shaggy Highland pony overtook our party and I careered after till Jenny Geddes, the clapped out old nag, tossed me into a bush in disgust.

Without prior warning the coach swerved into Leith Wynd and capsized, cowping us into the causie. Broken heads were in order but miraculously we were dazed, bruised but still walking. The coachman staggered off into the night still singing 'Saw ye my Maggie'. We released the poor mare, who was trembling with shock, and tethered her to a post till morning would bring equine relief. Then we took our separate ways home as best we might.

I was stiff on the stairs and by morning my right knee was like a balloon. Betty has it buffered with cushions and Wood set the kneecap straight at some cost to the poet. Damnably sore still but I think a bit reduced in size. I needs must disappoint the fair Mrs McLehose for tea. Shame, as I was looking forward to our better acquaintance. Will have to tantalise meantime, and convey the travails of the poet.

Very handsome letter from Mrs McLehose, tracking my gallantries at every turn.

Poet: *Never met a person in my life whom I more anxiously wished to meet again... shall not rest in my grave for chagrin... vexed to the soul I had not seen you sooner... determined now to cultivate your friendship with the enthusiasm of religion* [metaphorically, we hope]. *I cannot bear the idea of leaving Edinburgh without seeing you.*

Few can mine this vein so fluently, yet I am strangely taken with her and am not often mistaken in my partialities. So I told her in any case.

She: confesses a longstanding, earnest desire to make my acquaintance... has a strong presentiment that we should derive pleasure from the society of each other [my aim precisely]. She has fifty things to say to me. If I am prevented she will call with Miss Nimmo. She recognises my feelings – no, instincts – which have a powerful effect on her when [the warning note] under the check of reason and religion. [Clearly a woman of the west since what Edinburgh Miss would allow the spring to flow so freely]. She is devoted to poetry, an avid reader and tolerable judge. Encloses her own in response to my complimentary verse. The last is a solitary fly in otherwise soothing ointment – another Sappho *manqué*? But best of all is her close – *Will you let me know now and then how your leg is? If I were your sister* [could you not pretend?] *I would come and see you; but 'tis a censorious world this, and in this sense you and I are not of the world. Adieu. Keep up your heart, you will soon get well, and we shall meet. Farewell. God bless you. AM*

It is a meeting of hearts she proposes, a correspondence of poets. AM – O, sweet diversion. O, cursed knee.

Beugo kindly called to finish my visage. Hard to look dignified on one leg.

Stuck now in this drear attic. Stymied, stumped on all fronts. Surgeon Wood refuses further treatment, saying time and patience are the cures. No one calls; Smellie and Bob shamefaced or blaming me for the upset since I was the most sober, or least drunk. Left to my own company and Betty's ministrations.

Resolved to turn my confinement to some account. Even without Fennell, Jackson has a very decent set of players. Woods of course, Wilson, Bell, Wilson's wife, and *pièce de resistance* the summer seasoned: Mrs Siddons, Fanny Kemble and Mrs Jordan by yearly turns. But where are our Scotch dramas?

The Douglas, I concede – a fine vehicle for the female histrionic – and guid auld Ramsay's *Gentle Shepherd.* There's the sum.

Are we deficient in subjects, in story? Does everything have to come from London? Is the foreign and the exotic always to be courted, as if nonsense improves like brandy, when imported?

Themes to be put on stage: Bruce of course, and the incomparable Wallace, who makes Scottish blood flow through our veins. And loyal Jacobites, like Ochtertyre's tale of the Cameron who sheltered his Prince at the cost of exile.

Then what of Ossian and the Fingalian Band, the Blind Harper, and Cuchulainn wasted in weary war like Homer's Achilles?

Such are the dreams of a gallant nation now subdued but burning bright in better days.

Scene: *a drear dark cave, somewhere in the west. Discovered, the King of Scots, worn, shivering. Beside him – no outside – two or three faithful attendants, the loyal attendants. King groans, clutching the tattered cloak to his aching bones, pains stabbing at his chest.*

KING:
Alas that ever I mistook
My kin and Scottish kind
Who have proved strong and true
E'en at the cost of home –
And life itself – adamant
To the very last adversity
Of cruel oppressors' blows,
Yet sorely tried and wasted.

His mind turns as turn it must to his loyal wife and true born sister, both imprisoned in a cage like animals. So Edward Longshanks taunts all followers of Bruce by unnatural barbarities and suppression. Doubt assails him – can he continue with such a struggle?

KING:
This enterprise is all undone
Errors in ranks, hardship,
Battles lost before begun,
Ambush and skirmish, sole tactic
Gainst foes num'rous as trait'rous friends.
Here now in this last refuge
Shall I turn face to wall
And lower the sword arm
That cannot be raised more?
Defiance hopeless, head hung down.

Rough and sketchy, but will do for now.

Bruce averts his eye and gazes unseeing in the darkness, when suddenly his gloomy spirit is diverted, distracted by a humble spider clambering over rocky summits to launch

himself into an abyss no web could span, a chasm which
no thread could spin across. Down the spider goes but
swinging back into a crevice, catching without pause or
cease, he mounts once more to cast a fortune.

KING:
See the humble spider on his own account
Falls and slips again like me
His struggle unavailing
He does not surrender
Or give way to gloomy despairing.
See up, up he goes again
Defiant in the skyward scramble
Spinning once again across the chasm.
Try, try again, till my eye
Transfixed upon undaunted courage
Attains triumphantly his goal.

I could work this up for Woods to read, and solicit the
Manager. Scene by scene, speech by speech the drama can
be formed. Damn this leg, I need to move with the action.
For if the poet truly feels then every player can persuade
– the sentiment is true. Robert Burns is Robert Bruce
at bay, or on the field of Bannockburn addressing the
Scottish host. Or lying on a bed of aged pain, languishing
in weakness while my spirit longs to go on pilgrimage.
'Take my heart, brave Douglas, and carry it to Jerusalem.'
Drama worthy of the name of Bruce.

Or Stewart. What of the lovely, hapless Queen. She
could display the Tragic Muse in all her winsome glory.

'I was the Queen of bonnie France, but here I lie in
foreign bands.'

Yet still her heart is her own.

Is there no poet burning keen for fame
Will boldly try to gie us Plays at hame?

By divine permission of Dundas, Erskine Dean of
Faculty, and the assembled drawing rooms of Edinburgh.

Still if Jackson took it in hand. I must send out for a
manuscript book, or my journal will turn thespian. These
drublie days of winter and of my confinement shall be
dedicate to the national drama. As befits a Scottish Bard.

After four days neither walking nor moving except from
bed to seat and back, called in my old sour-faced friend
Glauber's salts. Passed my fifth between bed and pot. Knee
fiery; arse scadded.

Devoted to female correspondence. Let Peggy know of my
accident, as she might hear worse from others. Or think
the worst of me. Let tongues wag and a solitary capsizing
turns into a sunken fleet, one merry night a season of
dissipation.

If Peggy were here she would pour oil and balm into
my wounded soul. She is my angelic guardian.

Mrs McLehose encloses some more lines of verse with
her reply. She deprecates neatly, christening them rhymes
rather than poetry. But her aim is to converse as an equal.
So be it – I salute the female soul: my dearest madam
your lines are poetry and good poetry. I will write more
fulsomely tomorrow. Farewell, my poetess, may you enjoy
a better night's rest than I am likely to enjoy.

Contemplated a Bordeaux bottle but held off. Glauber
would protest and the poet must work tomorrow.

Miss Nimmo calls, most solicitous and sincere, though she could not conceal her anxiety to know what the poet thought of Mrs McLehose, her dear Nancy. I praise her friend's qualities of mind, her interest in literature, her grace of manner, and beg to know more about the lady.

It transpires that Mrs McLehose left her husband, a Glaswegian lawyer, due to his barbarous treatment of her and their children. For some time she was denied access to her little ones, but then she escaped to Edinburgh with them under her wing. Both her parents being dead, Nancy is dependent (this was conveyed by hints and the discreet yet persistent reference to money at which Edinburgh excels) on a small pension and on her cousin William Craig – another lawyer. Mark how this town sketches in the essentials of each situation: 'Burns, a talented man you know, but without income or position.'

I am warming to this lady of independent mind, if not of means. Rank is but the guinea's stamp and why should antique custom bind female virtue to male oppression? She lives it seems in General's Entry at Potterrow, a little refuge secured for her by the aforesaid Craig. I know of him since he writes sentimental twaddle in the periodicals and professes literature like a Man of Feeling *manqué*. But he has means. I thank Miss Nimmo for her confidence, and promise to write to Nancy, Mrs McLehose. Does Miss Nimmo know I have already written twice?

Tried to settle to my play, but the King of Scots wandered disconsolate in the wilds of Galloway. Dipped into MacPherson's *Ossian* to kindle my dramatic fire, but his high descriptive defies the stage. I cannot find a speaking character to put two firm Fingalian feet on the boards. Ossian's offspring are children of the mist to a last wraith.

Miss Nimmo mentions in passing her own brother William who is an Exciseman. Somebody told me last year that I should apply for an Excise Commission to supply my living – was it the good lady herself? Perhaps one of my Edinburgh acquaintance could speak for me to the Commissioners? The nearer I come to Ellisland, the leaner it looks.

Sent a note round to Ainslie begging his attendance. Without amusement I will turn drunken or mad, in either case out of my wits when I need them most.

Lord President Dundas died yesterday. The most powerful man of our time in Scotland. He held the reins of court and government, and his voice was always raised for order and the rule of law. Justice and poverty make ill-matched bedfellows.

Overwhelmed by visitors today. Surgeon Wood says I should write an elegy for the Lord President's passing. Let the Bard come to the bar, and deliver sentences or at least some stanzas.

The trouble with the playhouse is that it is in Edinburgh. The audience directs the drama and the players have to march in formation. No one looks to hear Scots spoken on the boards, yet in the country every passion, every shaft of wit, is borne on the mither tongue.

I am a bard o no regard
Wi gentle folks an aa that
But Homer-lik the glowran byke
Frae toun tae toun I draw that

What have I to do with President Dundas and Edinburgh's mourning? Black coats in dark kirks. Better a night at Poosie Nansie's with the tinkers to drink and dance and story. They gave me my beggars' wake – love and liberty! But my beggars' opera can neither be printed nor played. Yet they carry the people's drama, invisible to stage and page. So much for beggar poets and the death of kings.

The limb remains inert stretched out before me like a wooden appendage. But something in the rest of me is stirring. It may be my first conversion, albeit more dawning realisation than blinding light. The noon letter from Mrs McLehose is so far from gushing poetess as to check my every move to date.

She chides me for my romantic style, as if I were writing to some vain foolish woman or worse. She whom I address is a married woman: I stand rebuked. Then she pledges her friendship, of the heart and soul. In this realm she is a Duchess of Gordon, and were she a Duchess in means, her largesse would be no greater. A nobly independent sentiment which I of course approve – she has my measure there. In closing, she begs me not to write too often in case the exertion should hurt me. She however will continue to solace me in my confinement with an occasional letter.

How I have misjudged Nancy McLehose – she is a woman of character and I must rise to her level. But not yet. A delicate pause is essential to whet the female interest. Till I am more fitted for active service. Could the game be played as I have never played before? May she be an artist before whose feet the poet's garlands are freely lavished!

No communication this week from Creech. My indisposition gives him the perfect excuse for more delay. I can send messages but not hammer on his door for payment. He knows what is owing but evades his obligations at every turn. Mrs McLehose pledges me all her finer feelings while Creech denies me even a modest interim.

Edinburgh says I should refrain from calling in either debt, but I am not the retiring kind. I know what it is to go hungry, unlike Creech.

Dundas verses complete at last. Some commonplace and some hidebound but on the whole tolerable. Far from my best. Composed a letter though in my best style and sent it round by the hand of my esteemed surgeon. Solicitor Dundas, the son, was out, so Wood left the package.

A hackneyed subject, and besides the wailing of poets over great men's ashes is damnably suspicious. Let the Muses disdain my offering; I did what I could.

It is in the power of that clan to commission a cohort of poets or a legion of excisemen.

Another letter from Peggy. She does not forget sincere friends, God bless her.

Nothing ensues. Tomorrow. Tomorrow. Tomorrow. Retreat to the mental theatre in which I play all parts.

MacPherson is at the gallows. Half gypsy, half tipsy, he is at odds with society and condemned to hang on false testimony. He always lived on the outside by sharp dealing and pure artistry.

MACPHERSON:
There are some today have come to see me hang.

And some have come to buy my fiddle. But friends, before I part with my lovely companion, I'll break her through the middle.

The crowd draws back as he gestures fiercely.

MACPHERSON:
Little did my mother think when she first cradled me in her arms, that I would turn a roving boy and die on the gallows tree.

Then he puts the fiddle to his chin, playing like a madman and dancing in a last wild gypsy gyre.

Sae rantingly, sae dauntingly
Sae wantonly gaed he
He played a tune
And he danced it aroun
Ablow the gallows tree

Still whirling, he raises the fiddle in his hands and brings it smashing down on a boulder. Then he hangs. But what we remember is the dance and not the corpse. Every woman in the crowd felt him caress his violin.

Like Milton's Satan, he goes down with pride intact.
What Manager would stage it?
Everyone else defers and I bend the knee with them. Except perhaps the Deacon in his infernal lair. Yet what do I ken of the man. Ainslie hinted at some mystery or scandal but I ought not to rely on Bob's testimony. I feel as if he wants to make himself known to me in some way. For what purpose, and what could the poet offer up in return?

Crossed the room on crutches today. Mind much clearer. It's like the lifting of an Auld Reikie haar. The sun rises and the hares are leaping over a ploughed field. You can smell the fresh earth after a long-awaited shower. Why am I still here amongst these tight-packed tenements and shady closes? I belong in the country where Nature is never far from my side.

I am surprised to have taken Peggy's news so much in my stride. She has married Lewis Hay a rising banker. She has been secretly engaged to young Lewis since the summer; that is why she refused my proposal. Now she asks my understanding of her former constraint, and my continuing friendship. By God, she has both. Dear, dear Peggy, what a clearing of the air – heart and hand already promised. She has gained love and a living, and I wish her well on both counts.

Here, raised to Peggy! She hopes the best for me too – an honest living and a busy hearthside on my Dumfriesshire farm. Has anyone told her about Jean's new bairn?

An Excise Commission would forestall the farm and keep hunger from my door. These things must be attended. I can't feel easy when I spy that meagre, squalid spectre poverty. On her left hand she has iron-fisted oppression, on her right blasting contempt. Behind her stalks haggard famine. She broods on my path still, but I have withstood her wasting crew for many a day. My motto is 'I DARE'. To that I pledge my troth!

The worst enemy though is *moi-même*. Laid open to incursions of whim and caprice – the light banditti of imagination – while the heavy-armed regulars, wisdom and forethought, advance so very slow. I am a nation in perpetual war, divided between fear and desire.

What do you say to that, my old glass? I gallop across

on my oaken stilts to replenish you, nestling beside me. But I can take you or leave you, glassful by glass, o mellow ruby port. No port in a storm save thee. Enough to enjoy, not too much to destroy.

You know, my friend, there are only two creatures I envy in the wide world. An untamed horse on the steppes, and an oyster curled up on an abandoned shore. One can desire but not enjoy, while the other is beyond fear or want. Take my hand. Sound out the toast with steady resolve. To Peggy Chalmers – Mrs Hay – *Slainte!* As I said on the Braes of Atholl.

We have driven out the blue devils, as Fergusson would have it. Just mild indisposition, and the bottle has been set aside by Bob's decree. Now my whole mind can concentrate on the aching knee. No crutches today, but how long am I confined to this miserable room four floors removed from Mother Earth?

I sent out to have a set of Bible sheets bound for reading. Read through I mean like *Tristram Shandy* or *Tom Jones*. Let's see if this directory of texts still adds up to a book.

How to reply to Mrs McLehose?

First, I must confess to romantic weakness – my heart may have strayed. Second, is it a crime to be moved when you meet an unfortunate woman – one deserted by those who should protect, comfort and cherish? Especially when she is lovely of form and nimble in mind. This last addition might be pruned back. Third, she upbraids me. God rot the third. I need Betty's gruel, my pot, and some more sleep.

Later. Why is the poet wasting time on this letter when he should be practical? It will have to do as it is. I can command respect from long practice, but what will she make of it, the fair Nancy? I cannot somehow figure her clearly after all this epistolary guddling. Who knows what may chime? I could incorporate all my tacks into a fair copy in sequence – then she can choose the paragraph and style that please her best. I have no one to guide me here since even my journal rarely replies. Editing songs is easier than this flummery. Dispatch and be damned.

Have taken tooth and nail to the Bible. Got through the five books of Moses and half of Joshua by broth time. It really is a glorious book – and that before reaching the Psalms or the sublime chanting of Isaiah. Everything in life is here from the highest to the lowest: the faith of Abraham and the rape of Dinah, steadfast Noah and deceiving Jacob. Humanity as much as Divinity. Even Milton cannot command the epic sweep from Creation to Apocalypse. The Bible rehearses and reconciles us to the variorum of existence. The day passes *sans longueur*.

Hobbled to the window. Snow driving across the firth and shrouding Calton Hill.

Up in the morning's no for me
Up in the morning early
When aa the hills are covered wi snaw
I'm sure its winter fairly

Where did that come from? Perhaps someone sang it ower my cradle. Somebody's singing it still by the banks of Doon or Ayr. Give it a verse.

The burds sit chitterin in the thorn
A day they fare but sparely
And lang's the nicht frae e'en tae morn
I'm sure its winter fairly

I have been neglecting Johnson and his second volume; time to make amends.

That desolate hill reminds me of 'The Love Sick Maid'. The woman's lover has been hung at the Curragh of Kildare and she is left desolate. Summer is coming but her heart is wintry.

The winter it is past, and the summer comes at last,
And the small birds sing on every tree.
The hearts of these are glad, but mine is very sad,
For my lover has parted from me.
All you that are in love and cannot it remove,
I pity the pains you endure.
For experience makes me know that your hearts are
    full of woe,
A woe that no mortal can cure.

This has promise – more stanzas perhaps and it would do Johnson. She has the true and tender note that lassie of Kildare. Nature's beauty with the heart's lament. We must not neglect the Irish melodies.

What was the song Jean used to sing – 'The Northern Lass'.

Stay my charmer, can you leave me
Cruel, cruel to deceive me.
Can you go... can you go.

It's a Cumberland air, 'She Raise and Loot me in', but sung in Scotland and deserving some fresh words.

Have worked up my list. Completed seven by the time Betty brought me supper. I tried her out on 'The Northern Lass' but she threatened to turn skittish. Nae fule like an auld fule.

Judges, Samuel, Chronicles, Kings. Bloody tyrannies and righteous revolts. And old King David, he who slew Goliath and whom Jonathan loved, now chilled in life and limb, takes a virgin lassie to his bed. Anything to drive away the crawling spectre on his breast – death and judgement. In his mind's eye he sees Bathsheba in all her naked loveliness bathed, anointing her body with oils and perfumes.

O Prince's daughter, the joints of thy thighs are like
    jewels,
Thy navel like a round goblet that wanteth not
    liquor.

But the pintle lies shrunken below his belly like a wilted flooer. And the auld bear Saul rages and beats in his head, till he cries out for the balm of music and a girl's soft warm flesh. Jehovah and Jehoshaphat, those texts were rarely taken up in Mauchline's kirk. Old age slavering and pawing in his stews – bit close to home.

And what of me stuck in this den for ever, with only old Betty to attend me? Gloomy Psalms of repentance for my reading. Am I in hibernation that none visits or writes?

A king is served and flattered even in his dotage, but a poet is patronised and then shunned by fleeting fashion.

Poor Johnson is the honourable exception. He still

attends in motley and collects his dues in song. My contributions to his second volume are mounting up.

> Though mountains rise and deserts howl
> And oceans roar between;
> Yet dearer than my deathless soul
> I still would love my Jean.

Wearying in the solitary state of the Old Testament, I dipped into the New. Man of Sorrows – more brother than Saviour.

I have been in perpetual war with these doctrines of our reverend priesthood, that we are born slaves of iniquity wholly inclined to what is evil. Heirs of perdition, without spiritual filtration, the purgative chemistry of effectual calling, the oily medicine of sanctification – we cannot attain to virtue.

I hold the opposite, and conscience is my vindication. We come into the world ready to do good, until mixed with the alloy of selfishness, often disguised as prudence, the precious metal of our souls turns base currency. And that is why the gentler sex makes a more elegant impression of purity, goodness and truth than barbarian man.

Moreover a Benevolent Being broods over our earthly existence wishing the best for each and every one of us. Even Satan is of his party in the end. And that is why beyond our stinted bourne there is an immortal realm. If we lie down in the grave like a piece of broke machinery so be it – at least there is an end to pain and sorrow. But if that thing in us called mind or soul survives, then a mortal man conscious of acting an honest part among his fellows has nothing to fear, granting even that at times he may have been the sport of passions and instincts.

We go out to a great Unknown Parent who gave us these passions, and well knows their force. What other purpose in the giving? O Man of Sorrows, acquainted with grief. If not, then we are the playthings of cruel fate.

They brought the children to Jesus that he might bless them. She who stands to me in dear relation, who calls me Father, Daddy. Will her voice not be heard in the presence of that Being, author of our lives and breath? Some are already at his knee, abandoned in the helpless innocence of infancy.

Behold thou desirest truth in the inward parts
And in the hidden part thou shalt make me to know
    wisdom.
Purge me with hyssop and I shall be clean
Wash me and I shall be whiter than snow.
Sober and composed to rest.

Christmas Day. I stumbled down the stairs supported on both sides to family dinner. Happy scene as each returned from daily labour to gather round a welcoming hearth. Prayers offered up, warm fellowship, bright candlelight and savoury smells to enrich the appetite.

When will I have a hearth to call my own again – a place to gather my loved ones around me at peace, secure in a father's love? Composed a suitable reflection and then early to bed with little pain. Giving thanks for the child born in a stable, laid in the manger like an orphaned lamb in the cruel depths of winter.

Interleaved, a prayer.

O *thou great unknown Power, thou almighty God who has lighted up reason in my breast and blessed me with immortality, how often have I wandered from that order necessary for the perfection of thy works. Yet thou hast never left me nor forsaken me.*

Almost asleep when Bob and Willie arrived last night fully uproarious. They were marking the season and set on unstinting celebration of my recovery. I felt a sudden release from hermetic melancholy. Instead, I embraced joyful salutes to Yule, rodomontade unrestrained. Nothing can better the full, frank fellowship of men, Wassail, wassail.

Inconsolable by morning. *Tremore prostratus*. Lay inert till the short day sank once again into peaceful dark. Betty was hovering on the edge of vision. When I sat on the bed and sprayed my pot, there was an acid stink of cow piss.

By evening though I was on the mend and mobile. A letter arrived unannounced from Mrs McLehose. She now proposes a formal literary correspondence in which I will be Sylvander, the shepherd swain, and she Clarinda, a woodland nymph. This pastoral exchange will free us from tiresome carpings. Does the grime of daily existence constrain us? Then let us adopt the liberty of actors in a stage play.

My estimate of Agnes McLehose, nay, Clarinda, continues to soar. I must rise to this new challenge as Sylvander without totally surrendering Robert Burns. She takes me at my own value while at the same time setting the terms of our engagement. Has the poet met his match? A star has risen in Potterrow and I must go and worship, as long as I am detained in Edinburgh at least.

Fell asleep last night over Clarinda's poems, feeling that some supportive yet amending remarks might be well received. Rather tepid today, so sent a holding note – copying out her verses among my most valued pieces and so forth. Sylvander will write soon.

Is it not strange that someone of such great worth and natural gifts should be so unhappy? She is planning to leave town for a few days to visit in the country.

Gaining strength now every day, though still leaning on my crutches. I am invited to dine next door on Monday but can hardly venture out for the intense cold. As soon as I can get into a coach, I will call on Clarinda. Tomorrow I will lay the keel of a matchless epistolary vessel.

Much troubled with wind and relieved to sink back into a soothing daze.

Professor Gregory came round, genial and much concerned about my knee. Knowing his literary tastes, I gave him a sample of Clarinda's verse without revealing the author. He was very complimentary, but did he think they were mine? What an excellent fellow Gregory is – tall, generous, vigorous, and a true scholar. If only Edinburgh were full of his like.

Sat down seriously to the First Epistle. I was fluent, masterful, accomplished and could have gone on forever. But Betty came in with the soup.

By evening a hurried response arrived with a messenger from Potterrow. She writes in haste on the eve of departure. Took it to bed with me to mull over.

Interleaved: first letter to Clarinda, some loose pages.

I beg your pardon, my dear Clarinda, for the fragment scrawl I sent you yesterday. I really don't know what I wrote. A gentleman for whose character and abilities I have the highest regard called in just as I had begun the second sentence and I did not want the porter to wait.

I read several of my bagatelles to this much respected friend, and among them your lines which I had copied out. He began some criticisms on them all, yours included, when I informed him that they were the work of a young lady in this town. That I assure you made him stare and he protested that he did not believe any young woman in Edinburgh capable of such lines.

If you know anything of Professor Gregory you will doubt neither his ability nor his sincerity. I do love you, if possible, still better for having so fine a taste and talent for poetry. There, I have gone wrong again in my usual unguarded way, but you may erase the word and put esteem, respect or any other tame Dutch expression you please in its place.

You cannot imagine, Clarinda, (I like the idea of Arcadian names in a commerce of this kind), how much store I have set by your future friendship. I don't know if you have a just idea of my character, but I wish you to see me as I am. I am, as most people of my trade are, a strange will o wisp being, the victim of much imprudence and many follies. My great constituent elements are

pride and passion. The first I have tried to humanise into
integrity and honour, the second makes me a devotee
to the warmest degree of enthusiasm in love, religion or
friendship.

It is true that I have only seen you once, but how
much I formed upon that moment! Do not think I flatter
you, or have a design upon you, Clarinda – I have too
much pride for the one and too little cold contrivance
for the other. But of all God's creatures you struck
me with the deepest, strongest and most permanent
impression. And I say 'most permanent' knowing both
my prepossessions and my powers.

Why are you so unhappy, Clarinda? And why are so
many of our fellow creatures, unworthy to belong to the
same species, blest with all they can wish? You have a
hand open to give – why were you denied the pleasure?
You have a heart formed for all the most refined luxuries
of love – why was that heart ever wrung?

O Clarinda, shall we not meet in some yet unknown
state of being, where the hand of plenty will minister to
the highest wish of benevolence? And where the chill
north wind of Prudence will never blow over the flowery
fields of enjoyment? If we do not then human kind was
made in vain. I deserve most of the unhappy hours that
linger over my head; they are the wages of my labour.
But what unprovoked demon, malignant as hell, stole
upon the confidence of over trusting fate, and dashed
your cup of life with undeserved sorrow?

Let me know how long you will be out of town: I
shall count the hours till you inform me of your return.
Cursed propriety forbids you seeing me now, and as soon
as I can walk I must bid Edinburgh adieu. All this winter
– these three months past – what luxury of intercourse

I have lost. Lord, why are we born to meet with friends whose company we cannot enjoy, miseries that we cannot relieve.

   I am interrupted. Adieu, my dear Clarinda!
SYLVANDER

Sleepy today again and lazy. No business in hand, no Creech in sight, and Clarinda in rural retreat. I lay in bed and reviewed her letter once again.

She spurns my heartfelt sympathy since she is not unhappy but unfortunate. She still has her children, her friends, a modest competence, and freedom from guilt. Note a certain emphasis on the last. Would that the poet had half her resilience.

Religion has been her balm in every woe. Instead of scorning her tenets I should fall down and reverence even the shadow of true faith. She has me marked for an infidel – but when did I scorn? Is someone pouring Edinburgh's poison in her ear?

She will write again at her leisure. Who is she staying with in the country? And why has she not informed me?

Sweet sermoniser, mouthing delicious remonstrance. There is something in her tone revives my natural instinct. I want to hear her whisper cheek to cheek, lip to ear.

Postscript – I entreat you not to mention our correspondence to anyone on earth. Hence no forwarding address. Though her innocence is conscious, her situation is delicate. Never a truer word, Clarinda. Though my lips are sealed, my upright member tells a different tale.

O toppled towers of Ilium, your history began in such a moment. O gods, *delirium amoris*! Down, Hector, down.

Tomorrow is a dinner amidst distinguished company to mark the birthday of Prince Charles Edward Stewart. Loyalty to the true line of Scottish kings continues strong, and only this month His Royal Highness recognised Charlotte, his natural daughter by Clementina Walkinshaw, as Duchess of Albany. So he will not die without issue – the last of the blood is no longer the last – and all because of one glance across the candelabra at Bannockburn House as the Bonnie Prince led his army south. Thus history is made. I visited Bannockburn House in the summer and now I have made a song for Clementina's lovely daughter.

> My heart is wae and unco wae
> To think upon the raging sea
> That roars between her gardens green
> And the bonnie lass o Albanie

Today's task was a Birthday Ode for the dinner. Possibly the worst I have ever written. It creaks with the stage machinery of sentiment but it will serve, after the toasts have gone round and round again.

Only the Muse of song still attends me. I cannot write in Edinburgh without curbing passion, which is the wellspring of poetic impulse. Will anyone at this dinner draw a sword for Charlie?

> The injured Stewarts line are gone
> A race outlandish fill their throne
> An idiot race to honour lost
> Who knows them best despises most.

The defeat of despots and the overthrow of blind tyranny should be the objects of our study. Scotland may be a client kingdom now, but the instinct for liberty still pulses through our veins. One day the flame of freedom will once more burst forth with unrestrained fervour. Let the great ones beware – they know who they are – for the day and the hour will come – 'some blackened pride still burns inside this shell of bloody treason'.

Descended the stairs unaided and crutched round to the dinner. Oliphant of Gask, Lady Nairne's son, was in the company.

Toasts unbounded; Ode redounded.

On my return, faithful Betty tacked out from the kitchen and oxtered me back upstairs. Convivial salutes to 'Him Wha's Awa' sound in my ears like salvos of ordnance. Head clear as the frosty night beneath a maze of stars. Yet legs and ankles mutinous. Glad to regain quarters uncapsized. Recumbent, end night.

Woke late and lay feverish, listening to my heart beat and my blood pound like a hammer on the brain. Mouth dry and rancid. Suddenly I wanted to be at Mossgiel, or even Lochlea, up on a frosty morning and out into the yard to feed, milk and fodder. On Ne'erday, however hard the season, there's an extra handful to every beast with a blessing for the year ahead.

Decided to prepare a statement for Nancy setting out my follies along with the wisdom towards which I am still honestly striving. This would be a revision of my letter to John Moore laying my sum of experience before a benevolent friend and judge. But could not warm to the task; my pen scratched, stuttered to a halt.

The house was silent as a grave. As if everyone had left to keep an engagement elsewhere. Only myself for company till finally Betty brought the gruel.

Turned again to Clarinda's letter, and was drawn to her melancholy poem written outside the city walls on Bruntsfield Links. She felt utterly abandoned by the one whose nearest duty was to cherish her.

> Go on sweet bird and soothe my care
> Thy cheerful notes will hush despair
> Thy tuneful warblings void of art
> Thrill sweetly through my aching heart.

Gregory was much taken with this also. It has the true note of sorrow, elegantly expressed in the first stanza at least. Clipped the blackbird's wings and set her singing to an old Scots melody. Much improved all round.

Postponed writing my *Life* till tomorrow. How many times can a man explain himself, and to what purpose?

Later. Day lightened by a New Year letter from Clarinda, my rural mistress. Many happy returns of the season. Then after some literary nothings, she delivers the *coup de grâce*. While seeking to deflect amorous intention she achieves the contrary effect. Her intellectual command excites me beyond forbearance. She is my equal, an object of desiring *sans compeer*.

Interleaved: Clarinda's New Year letter.

Where worth unites with abilities it commands our love as well as admiration. Alas, they are too seldom found in one character! Those possessed of great talents would do well to remember that all depends upon the use made of them. Shining abilities improperly applied only serve to accelerate our destruction in both worlds.

I loved you for your fine taste in poetry long before I saw you. So I shall not trouble to erase that word applied in the same way to me. You say, 'there is no corresponding with an agreeable woman without a mixture of the tender passion'. I believe there is no friendship between people of sentiment and of different sexes without a little softness. But when kept within proper bounds it only serves to give a higher relish to such intercourse.

Love and Friendship are names in everyone's mouth, but few, extremely few, understand their meaning. Love – or affection – cannot be genuine if it hesitates a moment to sacrifice every selfish gratification to the happiness of its object. On the contrary, when it purchases one at the expense of the other it deserves to be called not Love but a name too gross to mention.

I therefore contend that an honest man may have a friendly prepossession for a woman whose soul would abhor the idea of an intrigue. These are my sentiments upon this subject; I hope they correspond with yours.

It is honest in you to wish me to see you 'just as you are'. I believe I have a tolerably just idea of your character. No wonder, since had I been a man I should have been you. I am not vain enough to think myself equal in abilities, but I am formed with a liveliness of fancy and strength of passion little inferior.

*Situation and circumstances have of course had
the effect on us that might be expected. Misfortune
has subdued the keenness of my passions, while the
adulation of success has nourished and inflamed yours.
Both of us are incapable of deceit, since we lack the
coolness to command our feelings. Art is what I could
never attain to, even in situations where a little would be
prudent. Nature has thrown me off in the same mould
just after you – we were born I believe in the same
year. Madame Nature has some merit by her double
handiwork – do you not agree?*

Seriously revised my *Life*. The letter to Moore has done
before, but it is in need of discreet pruning. This will be
for Clarinda's eyes only.

Once begun I wrote steadily through the day, finishing
strongly on religious principle – to counteract my atheistical
character. I will make a fair copy ready to leave in her
hands when we finally meet. For I cannot trust to those
fleeting moments to give a just impression of my poor
wayward self. She may already be stockaded about with
prejudice – a stout obstacle to any amorous enthusiast.

Day and evening have been consumed by honest labour.
This eased my melancholy, and I retired to rest satisfied
and hopeful despite all the troubles of a new year.

Rarely has a messenger been hailed with such impatience
and relief. Clarinda is back in town and in receipt of my
poetic offering. She sends me a gentle reproof – *talk not
of love, it gives me pain, for love has been my foe.* Instead

she proffers friendship's pure and lasting joys... but never talk of love.

The third stanza of her poem needs alteration, and there is a slight inaccuracy of rhyme in the second. But both are easily mended. Set to 'The Banks of Spey' this might adorn Johnson's *Musical Museum*. I hazard though one more stanza.

> Your thought if love must harbour there
> Conceal it in that thought
> Nor cause me from my bosom tear
> The very friend I sought.

Could I venture round now to Potterrow in a coach without hurting myself, Clarinda sweetly enquires. How much can two people pass between them without seeing each other?

By sedan chair I may come, borne by cadies whose every breath is sober, steeled against satiric shafts. If I could be sure of finding you at home...

I will spend from five to six o'clock with Mrs McLehose. And one other evening before I leave town for good. My mind misgives as to how and when to present my autobiography.

He who sees Clarinda as I have done and does not love her, deserves to be damned for stupidity. He who loves and would injure her shall be cast into the fiery furnace.

Adieu, Clarinda, till I meet my Nancy once again in the flesh. Sweet dream, adieu.

EDINBURGH
January 1788

A History of Myself

by
Robert Burns

Marked with some Emendations
and Interleaved at the back
of the Journal

I HAVE TAKEN the resolution to give you a history of myself. You have done me the honour to interest yourself warmly in the poet and his works, and I think that a faithful account of what character of a man I am and how I came by that character may amuse you.

I will give an honest narrative though I know it will be at the cost of being frequently laughed at. For though I esteem wisdom like a Solomon, I have often turned my eyes to behold madness and folly, and joined hands with them in intoxicating friendship. If after scanning these pages you think them trifling or impertinent, only consider that the poor author penned them with twitching qualms of conscience that perhaps he was doing what he ought not to do, a predicament that he has found himself in more than once.

I have not even the most distant pretensions to be what the heraldic guardians call a gentleman. Almost every name in the kingdom can claim some mention in the Lord Lyon's annals but gules, purpure and argent have disowned me.

My ancestors rented land in Aberdeenshire from the noble Keiths of Martial, and had the honour to share their fate. By honour I do not refer to party principle, but their willingness to accept ruin and disgrace for what they sincerely believed to be the cause of their God and King, the Royal House of Stewart.

I mention this because it threw my father on the world at large, where after many years' wanderings and labour he gained a large share of observation and experience to which I have always been indebted. I have met with few people who understood men and their manners as well as my father. Yet stubborn, ungainly integrity along with headlong, ungovernable irascibility are disqualifying circumstances in the world. So I was born a very poor man's son.

For the first seven years of my life my father was the gardener to a small estate near Ayr. Had he continued in that situation I would have gone off to be raised as a farm boy in the neighbourhood. But it was his dearest wish to keep his children under a father's eye till they could discern between good and evil. So, with the assistance of his master, he ventured himself on a small farm in the area.

As a child I was noted for retentive memory, a stubborn, sturdy something in my disposition, and a blind enthusiasm for all things religious and imaginative. Though I cost the schoolmaster some thrashings, I was an excellent English scholar and aged ten, a critic in substantive verbs and particles.

In my infant days, though I was by no means a favourite, I owed much to an old maid of my mother's, remarkable for her credulity and superstition. Betty Davidson had the largest collection in the county of tales and songs concerning devils, ghosts, fairies, brownies, witches, warlocks, spunkies, kelpies, elf candles, dead-lights, wraiths, apparitions, cantraips, giants, enchanted towers, dragons and other trumpery. These wonders cultivated latent seeds of poesy, yet had such an effect on my imagination that to this hour in my nocturnal rambles I keep a sharp lookout, though nobody could be more sceptical in these matters than the poet.

The earliest composition I remember taking pleasure in was Addison's hymn beginning 'How are thy servants blessed, O Lord.' I still recall one half stanza which caught my boyish ear: 'For though in dreadful whirls we hang, High on the broken wave'. I met these pieces in Masson's

English Collection, one of my school books.

The first two books I ever read in private were the *Life of Hannibal*, and the *History of Sir William Wallace*. They gave me more delight than any books I have read since. Hannibal gave my young ideas such a turn that I used to strut up and down in raptures after the recruiting drum and pipes. The story of Wallace poured a Scottish prejudice in my veins which will boil along there till the floodgates of life shut in eternal rest.

My closeness to Ayr was a great advantage. I formed many attachments and friendships with other youngsters who possessed superior privileges to mine. Youngling actors busy with the rehearsal of parts, they were destined to feature on a stage behind whose scenes I would be a menial drudge. In these green years the young noblesse and gentry do not have that sense of unbridgeable distance between themselves and their raggèd playfellows. It takes a few dashes into the world to give the fledgling Great Man a proper disregard for the mechanics and peasantry around him.

However these young superiors never insulted the clouterly appearance of my ploughboy carcase, both ends of which were exposed to all the rigours of the seasons. They lent me storybooks, one of which helped me to a little French. Then bit by bit I experienced the sore affliction of partings as one by one they dropped off for the East or West Indies.

But soon I was called to more serious evils. My father's generous old master died. Our farm proved a ruinous bargain, and as if to clinch our misfortune we fell into the hands of a factor who was as merciless as he was unjust. My father had already been advanced in years when he married and I was the eldest of seven children. Worn out by early hardship and unfit for labour, his spirit was easily irritated, yet not broken.

We retrenched expenses, dispensed with hired labour, and lived very poorly. I was a skilled ploughman for my young years, and my nearest brother Gilbert could drive the plough, harvest and thresh with me. The novel writer might view these scenes as pastoral, but in truth I combined the gloom of a hermit with the unceasing toil of a galley slave. Life was accompanied by hurts, strains and miserable soakings. My heart still boils with indignation at that tyrant factor's threatening letters which reduced all of us to tears.

It was in my fifteenth year that I first committed the sin of rhyme. The country custom was to couple a man and a woman together, reaping and binding. My partner in that fifteenth autumn was just one year younger. My poor English does her no justice for in Scotch she was a bonnie, sweet, sonsie lassie.

Unwittingly she initiated me into that delicious passion which, in spite of bookworm philosophy and acid disappointment, I still hold to be the first of human joys and the dearest delight of our earthly life.

I never told her that I loved her, so how she caught the contagion I know not. I did not really know myself why I liked to loiter with her when we came home together in the evening from the fields, why her voice made my heart quiver like a harp, why my pulse beat with a rat-tat-tat when I gently fingered over her hand to pick out the thorns and thistles.

She also sang sweetly and it was her favourite reel that I tried to set to rhyme. I did not imagine that I could make verses like printed ones – written by men who knew Latin and Greek. But when I heard her sing a country song I felt that I could make something of the same kind. So began for me love and poetry, which till this last year have been my highest enjoyment.

My father struggled on till he reached the freedom of his lease, when he took a larger farm ten miles further out into the country. This new bargain put a little ready money in his hand for the first few years. We lived comfortably until a lawsuit between us and the landlord tossed and whirled my father into the vortex of litigation. Then consumption kindly stepped in to snatch him from incarceration and convey him to that bourne where the wrecked cease from trembling and the weary are at rest.

During this time I was still the most ungainly being in the parish. My knowledge was had from school texts and the periodicals. Pope's poetry, some plays of Shakespeare, Dickson on Agriculture, Stackhouse's *History of the Bible*, Taylor's *Doctrine of Original Sin*, Allan Ramsay's *Works*, Hervey's *Meditations* and *Select English Songs*, were the full extent of my reading. I pored over that song collection, driving my cart or walking to the field, line by line, verse by verse, carefully dividing the tender and sublime from the affected.

In my seventeenth year I went to a country dancing school to give my manners a brush. My father took against these assemblies but I continued in absolute defiance, which I repent to this hour. As I said before, my father was prey to strong passions, and from this rebellion he took an aversion to me, which I believe was one cause of the dissipation I became party to. I say dissipation, but only in comparison to the sobriety of country Presbyterians of the old Covenanting kind. Whatever thoughtless whims distracted me, ingrained piety and virtue never failed to point the path of innocence.

The great misfortune of my life was not to have an aim. My early stirrings of ambition were like the blind gropings of a Cyclops round the walls of his cave. I felt bound by my father's situation to perpetual labour. My only access to livelihood opened onto niggard economy or the chicanery of bargain-making. I could not squeeze myself through that narrow aperture.

Meanwhile my strong sociability, native hilarity, a pride of observation and remark, a hypochondriac taint that caused me to flee solitude, my reputation for bookish knowledge, a certain wild, logical talent, and a strength of thought masquerading as good sense, all combined to make me a welcome guest and companion. So where two or three gathered together, there was I in the midst of them.

But beyond all other impulses, my heart was tinder, eternally lit up by some goddess or another. Sometimes I was crowned with success, sometimes mortified by defeat. At plough, scythe or reaping hook, I feared no competitor and defied want. But I spent the evenings pursuing my own desire. The very goose feather in my hand seems instinctively to know the well-worn tenor of my imagination – the fervent theme of my song. Only with difficulty is it prevented from tracing the amours of my compatriots, lowly denizens of farmhouse and cottage. The grave doctors of science and religion name these follies, but to the sons and daughters of labour they are matters of the most serious import. To them the ardent hope, the stolen interview, the exchange of love, and the tender farewell constitute the finest and most delicious part of their existence.

My life flowed on in much the same course till my twenty-third year. *Vive l'amour* and *vive la bagatelle* were my sole principles of action. But the addition of two more bosom companions gave me great pleasure. *Tristram Shandy* and *The Man of Feeling* were my especial favourites. Poetry was still the darling of my walks but it was only a humour of the hour. Usually I had half a dozen or more pieces on hand, taking up and laying them down as it suited my inclination or fatigue. Once lighted my passions raged like so many devils till they got vent in rhyme. Then conning over my verses like a spell soothed all into quiet. None of the rhymes of those days were in print – apart from the 'Winter Dirge' – until James Johnson's *Scots Musical Museum* gave them a home.

That twenty-third year marked the first great crisis of my life – the first at any rate arising purely from my own initiative. Partly from whim and partly that I wished to find another means of living, I joined with a flax dresser in the neighbouring town of Irvine. My ambition was to learn his trade and carry on the business of manufacturing and retailing flax.

This turned out badly. My partner was a scoundrel whose trade was mingled with that of theft. And to finish the whole sorry tale, while we were welcoming in the New Year, by the drunken carelessness of my partner's wife, our shop was burnt to ashes, leaving me, like the proverbial poet, without sixpence to my name.

I was obliged to surrender the business, at the very moment when the clouds of misfortune were lowering over my father's head. Darkest of these was the consumption that was visibly wasting him. Then to crown all, a *belle fille* whom I adored and who had pledged her soul in the field of matrimony, jilted me at her father's instigation. Our engagement was spurned and denied in mortifying circumstances.[*Sentence scored out.*] My hypochondriac complaint was so inflamed that I spent three months in a diseased state of mind and body.

Nonetheless I learned something of town life from this episode. And I formed a close friendship with a young man, the first human being whom I had really known in their inner clothing. Though himself a hapless son of misfortune, this young gentleman's mind was fraught with courage, independence, magnanimity, and every manly noble virtue. He turned my mind, I loved him, I admired him, and I strove to imitate him.

And in some measure I succeeded. I had the pride before and the passion but he taught them to flow through proper channels. His knowledge of the world was vastly superior to mine and I was attentive to all his lessons. Moreover, he was the only man I ever saw who was a greater fool than myself when woman was the presiding star. Yet he spoke of fashionable failings which I had hitherto regarded in horror with levity. Here at any rate his friendship did me a mischief, and in consequence soon after I resumed the plough, I had to welcome a child whose mother refused me marriage, though I stoutly maintained the duties of fatherhood.

When my father died, his worldly all went to the rapacious hellhounds that growl in the kennel of misnamed justice. But we made shift to scrape a little money with which to keep us together. My brother and I took the neighbouring farm of Mossgiel on hopeful terms. Gilbert lacks my harebrained imagination as well as my social disease; in good sense and every sober qualification he is my better by far.

I entered in on this farm on a flood-tide of resolution. I read agricultural books, I calculated crops, attended markets and in short put the Devil, the World and the

Flesh behind me. I believe I would have matured soon into a wise husbandman. But the first year from buying bad seed, and the second from a late harvest, we lost half of our crops. This overset all my application, and I retuned 'like the dog to his vomit, and the sow that was washed by wallowing in her mire'.

I had all but given up poetry excepting some religious pieces. But suddenly encountering Fergusson's Scotch poems, I strung anew my rustic lyre with emulous vigour. I now began to be known in the neighbourhood as a maker of rhymes. At this time polemical divinity had set the country half-mad. And the first of my poetic offspring to be handed round for admiration was a burlesque lamentation on the quarrel between two Reverend Calvinists – *dramatis personae* in my 'Holy Fair'.

It met with a roar of applause on a certain side of both clergy and laity, but also raised a hue and cry of heresy against me which has not ceased to this hour.

'Holy Willie's Prayer' next made its appearance. This is one of my best known pieces yet never printed nor ever to be printed while breath remains in this corporeal frame.

It alarmed the Kirk Session so much that they held three special meetings to look over their righteous artillery and decide if any of it could be discharged against profane rhymers.

Unluckily for me the aftermath of my failed betrothal left me on another flank point blank within range of their heaviest metal. [*Sentence scored out.*] It was a shocking affair which I cannot yet bear to recollect in all its particulars. I was close to losing my bearings so shaken was I in the very hold of reason. Threatened at law, I gave up my share of the farm to Gilbert and made what little preparation I could to sail to Jamaica.

[*Paragraph blotted out.*]

Before leaving my native land for ever, I determined to publish my poems. I weighed my productions as impartially I thought they had merit. What though their true measure should never reach the ears of a poor slave driver or some hapless victim of that inhospitable clime? I would still leave to the world a critical reckoning.

It has always been my opinion that the great unhappy mistakes and blunders, both in a rational and a religious view, of which we see thousands guilty, are owing to mistaken notions of our selves. To know myself had all along been my constant study. I weighed myself alone; I balanced self with others; I gauged every inch of ground I occupied both as man and poet. I studied assiduously where Nature's design seemed to have intended the lights and shades in my character. I was pretty sure that my efforts would meet with some applause, but at the worst the Atlantic roar would deaden any voice of censure. The novelty of the West Indies would dull any sense of unjust neglect.

I threw off six hundred copies of my poems in Kilmarnock. I had subscriptions for three hundred and fifty of them, and my vanity was highly gratified by the reception I met with from the public. Besides I pocketed nearly twenty pounds with all expenses deducted.

This arrived just in good time as I had been about to indent myself to bonded labour for want of money to pay my passage. As soon as I became master of nine guineas I reserved a passage on the first ship to sail for the Indies. I took a last farewell of my few friends; my chest was on the road to Greenock; I had composed the last song I would ever measure in Caledonia. When a letter from Dr Blacklock, your near neighbour at Potterrow, overthrew all my schemes: he raised poetic ambition beyond my wildest imaginings.

The Doctor said that I would meet with every encouragement for a second edition in Edinburgh. Fired by this encouragement, I posted for the capital without a single acquaintance in the town, or a single letter of introduction in my pocket. You may imagine the cold shock of my arrival in this teeming anthill of self-absorbed busyness.

But the baneful star so long in its zenith now revolved to a nadir. The providential care of a good God placed me under the patronage of the Earl of Glencairn. I entered a new world, mingling among all classes of men and women. The interest of my benefactors, not least that very Mackenzie who had authored my *Man of Feeling*, secured the new edition – to what effect you can judge for yourself.

For some months since I have been rambling over the country, partly to settle some business of the new edition and partly to make the poet's face more familiar. But above all to garner inspiration from the scenes and melodies of Caledonia – 'that I for poor auld Scotia's sake, some useful plan or book could make, or sing a song at least'.

Now I have returned to Edinburgh to await the pleasure of my printer Mr Creech, and consider my future in life. But, my dear Clarinda, you are right: a friendly correspondence goes for nothing unless we disclose our undisguised feelings. I hope that I have shown you something of myself. Yet my heart is wounded by the loss of one who was nearest to myself in soul and body. I cannot tell you more by letter.

Your sentiments please me for their intrinsic merit, as well as because they are yours, which I assure you is high commendation to me. Your religious emotion I revere, and if you have on some suspicious evidence, from some lying oracle, learnt that I despise or ridicule so sacred a matter as real religion, then you have much misconstrued your friend.

My own definition of worth is short: truth and humanity respecting our fellow creatures, reverence and humility in the presence of that Being – my Creator and Redeemer – who I have every reason to believe will one day be my Judge.

I can easily enter into the sublime satisfaction that your strong imagination and keen sensibility must derive from religion, particularly when a little overshadowed by misfortune. But I admit myself unable, without a marked grudge, to watch Heaven totally engross so amiable, so charming a woman as my friend Clarinda. I should be well pleased if circumstance put it in the power of somebody, Happy Somebody, to divide her attention with all the delicacy and tenderness of an earthly attachment.

Yours etc, SYLVANDER

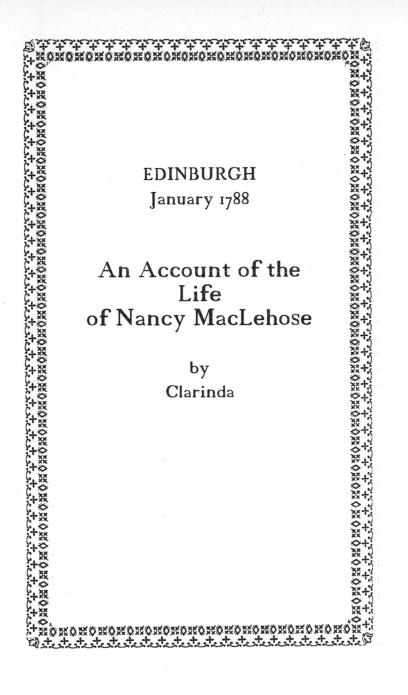

EDINBURGH
January 1788

An Account of the
Life
of Nancy MacLehose

by
Clarinda

SYLVANDER'S ACCOUNT OF himself has moved and enlightened me. There is pride and passion in that tale yet also the struggle for a tolerable *modus vivendi*, whatever cruel blows life inflicts on us. I recognise that honest endeavour and the courage it requires, since your struggle is companion to mine.

It is generous of you to wish that I see you 'just as you are'. I believe I have a true sense of your nature. No wonder for as I said before, had I been a man, I would have been you. Do you recoil at the thought?

I wish to repay your confidence by laying out the story of my life. Not as to a stranger, but to a friend bound by sympathy, respect and a full measure of affectionate understanding.

I was born and brought up in Glasgow in the same two storeys of a tall tenement in the Saltmarket. My father was a doctor and I had one older sister, Margaret, who was my constant playmate and companion. All my earliest memories are coloured by the presence of my beloved mother. She was a loving and devoted soul; each one of her small family occupied a large room in her heart, yet there was always space for relations, neighbours, friends, and for the poor or sick who came often knocking at my father's door.

My mother had been brought up in a manse. Reverend John MacLaurin, her father and my grandfather, was minister at Luss and then at St David's, Ramshorn, where he ministered often in Gaelic to Glasgow's Highlanders. His father in turn was minister at Kilmodan so they were all Gaelic speakers, and once I believe the MacLaurin Chiefs of Tiree.

From the outset my mother was imbued with a profound sense of religion, and though never stern she founded her life on a bedrock of principle. I rarely saw her angry but her disapproval, spoken or unspoken, was compelling. My father was liberal in outlook, yet he always respected her principles as part of the deep and true bond which united them. I would run to his knee for a story, or to hers for comfort, but every morning and evening she joined our hands in prayer.

We ourselves were often in need of a doctor. I was a feeble infant and my hold on life was uncertain. I believe that I had a difficult birth, and my mother endured a long convalescence with frequent illness. It seems that Margaret and I were always aware of a shadow lingering beneath our happiness. Gradually as we grew, our mother became weaker. Night after night our father held her in his arms, till eventually she slipped away to a better place.

I was much younger than you when your father lost his hold on an unkind world. Yet I understand your feelings and share them completely. Would that I had kept more closely to her teaching and guidance through my giddy youth. But I am running ahead of myself. What I do clearly remember from these days are snatches of prayers and hymns, including that lovely verse of Addison's which is also your earliest memory.

Glasgow was a bustling place in which to grow up. Our lofty lodgings were just south of where Trongate, High Street and Saltmarket meet in a cacophony of traffic, traders and loiterers. The Toun College – or University as they prefer – was further up towards the Cathedral, that sublime relic of more solemn and grander days. The Tolbooth Court and Jail stood at the junction of all these busy routes. Beggars mingled with professors and lawyers with common hawkers. The streets of Glasgow level all to an equal degree.

When we were little, our mother denied us the street and insisted on us playing inside. Only common ragamuffins were given the run of the stair and the filthy causeways. However, after she passed away we broke out from under our father's more negligent hand. We had the run of the town, through narrow alleys into the Gallowgate or down onto the Green, where the great river crawled slowly by and massed ranks of washing lay out to dry. Every day we underwent the penance of private lessons, but chafed at the leash till we could break free.

I was by all accounts a sturdy youngster once I had outgrown my infant ills. Often at the head of games, I ordered my playmates about and spoke out even in adult company. In the street we chanted 'Here we go by the jingo ring' and 'Round the merry-ma-tanzie'. But when my father came wearily along, carrying his surgical bag, we quickly retreated to play the part of polite little misses receiving company at home. I am told that my complexion was always pale but that with any excitement or exertion my pallid tones flushed warmly red.

Naturally we soon became more self-conscious and restrained. This was not though the chiding of our elders – our aunts and uncles or our dear, indulgent parent – but our own inner prompting. We consulted the mirror, compared appearances and began to consider how the world might regard us. We were not vain, nor did I, at least, have any cause since my nose turned up and my chin curved inwards. Yet we were soon intensely aware of appearance.

Suddenly the romance of street urchins had faded. We were young ladies in waiting, and dressed in shawls with matching bonnets we sallied out to call on friends. Up the stairs we went to try our hand at polite conversation, supping tea and mutely studying the ornaments and furnishings of every house. In truth, our main interest was the appearance of our peers, male or female, and the performance often dissolved in giggles or irreverent mirth.

By this time my father had been appointed town surgeon of Glasgow. Every day he laboured to relieve fever, abscess, flux and mental perturbation. Disease and distress were evident on every side, yet could have been invisible for all the impression made on us. Our elders strove to bind the wounds while we went gaily by with all the light-headed arrogance of youth. Even at Sunday service in my uncles' kirk, we struggled to suppress our giggling.

All this levity was truly innocent, but of course we were growing into young women. My first experience of the tender emotion came on a visit to our MacLaurin cousins in Edinburgh. They were much older than us except for William the youngest who was nearer to me in age. He volunteered to show me the sights and I fancied he had taken a special fondness for me, young as I was.

We walked out to the Castlehill, to the romantic ruin of Holyrood, onto Arthur's Seat, and down to the woodland paths by the Water of Leith. As day followed day in this brief idyll, I saw everything through the balm of his gentle companionship. I think it was William who first took my hand in his. A delicious yet chaste sensation invaded me; I seemed to walk on air in a cloud of diffused, radiant light. What a gentleman he was – delicate, protective and content to bask in my admiration. Within the year, he was dead of a fever.

I have not thought of William for many years, but the account, Sylvander, of your first gleaning and the lass of that early harvest, brought him back to mind as if it were yesterday. What tricks memory can play. Nothing can ever replace that first sublime softening.

You seem to have known this feature of my character intimately, and consequently entrusted me with all your faults and follies. The description of your first love scene delighted me. Our early love emotions are surely the most exquisite. In later years, my dear Sylvander, we may acquire more knowledge and more discrimination of sentiment, but none of these qualities can yield such rapture as the first delusions of the heart.

No more of these idle recollections. It was not my emotions but Margaret's that occupied our full attention. She was approaching the age when young Scottish women of good family are expected to wed. But with whom? I began a habit – continued for some time thereafter – of listing Glasgow's eligible young batchelors, with appendices for Dumbarton, Greenock and all points beyond. Note the 'young'. Both Meg and I were resolved not to be purchased by the wealthy like prime stock at a country fair. There are traces in this precious Scotland, Sylvander, of more barbarous times, for Woman at least.

There had been no definite conclusion to my researches till one afternoon we were visitors at our Craig cousins in St Andrew's Square and a Captain James Kennedy of Kailzie and Auchterfardle came calling. He was a slender Highlander with fair colouring, a courteous manner and keen hazel eyes beneath his smooth brow. Mentally I added him to my catalogue without hesitation. But it was too late. As we waited for the tea to arrive Margaret whispered to me that here was the man she wanted to marry.

How to proceed? With our mother departed and our father distracted, it would not be proper for a young man to visit alone, but since there were two of us... He arrived promptly and Bella our maid, cook and woman of all work, ushered him in to the drawing room. We rose to our feet, beribboned and becurled. He bowed; we bobbed. Holding his sword gracefully at an angle, the Captain sat down, while we perched ourselves on the settle edge. The weather was certainly much clearer since the rain had passed over, perhaps even seasonable.

Stilted talk progressed to more convivial lines. He laughed and joked about his time as a student, his lodgings near the Cathedral, night time japes by the Necropolis, and the Gallowgate taverns. Margaret hung on every word, teasing now and then to draw him out further.

'Will ye hae the tea noo?' Bella's interruption came as a surprise to everyone. Margaret handed round the cups and I followed in train with sugared biscuits.

Within weeks we were speculating feverishly on a wedding date. Father was informed, complaining mildly at being the last to know. On 1st May 1771, Margaret and James were married. My principal mission in life had been accomplished. Yet I still had my list. I was now thirteen years of age.

Should I regret these carefree times? Had my mother lived things would surely have been different. Yet there was an innocence in my high spirits. My invitations increased till every family of merit claimed acquaintance with 'pretty Miss Nancy'. There is a familiarity in Glasgow society not practiced in Edinburgh. Did that redound to my discredit? Not at all. I was a bright spark amidst the stour of business and the bleak squalor of poverty. A butterfly fluttering through a rapacious jungle.

Of course I was teased, but I gave as good as I received. Friends said I was a walking encyclopaedia of unattached young gentlemen. One such was James McLehose, a lawyer's agent, whom I first sighted at a soirée standing in a corner, slender, tall and dark, leaning over the daughter of our hostess. He caught my eye, but no more. If only it had rested there. As things transpired, I had come under his keen notice.

Conceive our delight when Margaret announced that she was expecting a baby. After all our losses, here was a great gain. Is there not always joy at the first signs of a new life? Though if the amours of country life run without restraint, then perhaps such first showing is not always welcome?

Our pleasure was unalloyed. We talked continually about the baby's clothes and toilette. A blushing and bashful Captain James was constantly engaged in discussion on the choice of name, the likelihood of boy or girl, and so forth. Even my poor father looked up with a fresh interest in life.

A few short months later, Margaret died giving birth to a stillborn child. I had lost a sister who was also my best friend and closest companion in life. On a drear day of grey rain, Margaret was laid to rest by her heartbroken husband and father.

I sank into the slough of sadness and can hardly account for my next twelve months. Has it ever been so with you, Sylvander? Is such the effect of melancholy? I suppose that I continued to eat, sleep, breathe and make social calls, but drained of spirit, I was the empty shell of my former person.

Did my father notice my condition in the depths of his own depression? Or was he eventually shocked into action by my wan appearance, my efforts to put on an empty show of bravado? Whatever the cause he decreed that his nearly fifteen-year-old daughter should be delivered to a recently established school in Edinburgh where young ladies were finished by spinster ladies who were anything but young.

That is why, before eight o'clock on a fine, fresh morning in May, only three years after Margaret's marriage, I was standing outside the Black Bull, awaiting the departure of an Edinburgh coach. Was I in any way conscious that the fates were about to take a hand in my own future? I think not. I was excited at the prospect of Edinburgh, but oblivious to everything except my father's clumsy farewells.

The stable boys were bringing out the horses when he remarked that apart from the young man standing in the inn doorway, there were no other passengers for that day. I glanced over and immediately recognised James McLehose. I said nothing as my father handed me into the empty coach and departed, relieved no doubt to fulfil his parental duties while avoiding the actual moment of leaving.

It was a ten-hour journey yet I can honestly say that, potholes notwithstanding, the time flew by. Mr McLehose was a reserved and rather formal young man. Though I had noticed him and I knew that he had noticed me, he had not presented himself at our house in the Saltmarket or sent cards and flowers like so many other venturesome gallants. But in order to have me to himself, he had ascertained the day of my journey to Edinburgh and booked all the other seats in the coach.

I flattered myself that on that journey he told me everything about himself. Beyond that, there were the dark eyes and fine features, the slender frame. I was much taken with James McLehose, gave him my confidence, and encouraged him to what end you, Sylvander, know well.

But have you never yourself entered into an attachment, carried on the wings of instant attraction? And lived to rue the day. But again, I anticipate, for this is designed to be a narrative of my life in your style and manner.

The Misses MacRae maintained their finishing establishment on the south side of the town adjacent to the Meadows, a broad green sward which had been drained and laid out to gardens some years before. To the east were the old lands of Kirk O Field where Queen Mary's Darnley met his murderous end; to the north was the University; to the west Heriot's Hospital, and to the south the gently rising grounds of Sciennes and Marchmont. From this higher vantage, Arthur's Seat was visible surveying all beneath.

We were sixteen young misses in total, and as high-spirited and bold a covey as ever hunter shook from the woodland branch. Yet the Misses MacRae managed, without tyrannical suppression, to take us through several course of improvement. We learned deportment and manners, conversation skills and the protocols of rank. I was unaccustomed to such solemn distinctions and saw little worth or purpose in them.

We also learned needlework, drawing, a little French and the art of composing letters or even a stanza of verse. I excelled in literary exercise, discovering for the first time something for which I had a special aptitude. The ladies had a good stock of poetic texts as well as new verse editions, which I was allowed to borrow and peruse at my leisure. We were also encouraged to keep commonplace books recording our favoured lines, observations and compositions. So began for me the custom of journal-keeping which has never left me, as well as a desire for correspondence of the intimate and confiding sort. As you yourself aver, what is the point of letters if we do not communicate our inner feelings, the true tenor of our souls? In that, Sylvander, I know I have your understanding and approbation.

But the great discovery of that second Edinburgh sojourn was the novel. These volumes were not displayed in the school's modest library. But the younger Miss MacRae was an avid collector. When I had gained her confidence, she lent me one by one *Pamela*, *Clarissa*, *Tom Jones* – all with vigorous head shaking admonitions – *Amelia*, and your Mackenzie's *Man of Feeling*.

O, the exquisite sensations of living through these crises and entanglements. The long exchange of letters, the swinging pendulum of honour and dishonourings, malevolent design overcoming or thwarted by determined virtue. And through all the sway of sentiment: lives lived for the fullness of the heart or its tragic folly. A new world was opened to me through these pages, yet it was also strangely familiar territory, as if this had always been my true inheritance. Here I chime, Sylvander, with all your early reading, and the birth therefrom of your sentient being. If only we had become acquainted at that time and had been able to share our tremulous explorations by letter and by conversation. We would have become our own novel creation!

Cultivation of heart and pen were the chief gains of my schooling. As to our social grooming, I remained indifferent; my attitudes to birth, rank and fortune were truly unfashionable. I despise people who pique themselves on either, but especially the former. Something should be allowed to bright talents or even external beauty since these belong to our selves; a mere accident of birth cannot confer essential merit. I would not then or now take anyone of a vulgar uncultivated mind to my bosom whatever their station. But someone possessed of natural genius and improved by diligent education is a welcome friend, however mean their extraction.

Are we not all the offspring of Adam? Have we not one God, one Saviour, one hope of immortality? I did not find anyone among my fellows who shared this philosophy – it was not accepted doctrine in the school of MacRae! On returning to Edinburgh, I do not find it any more in fashion now.

The time came for going home to Glasgow. I had received regular letters from Mr McLehose, short and sweet epistles, and whenever I was between terms we always contrived to meet. He was shy but intense in his feelings, and persistent. He became part of my inner private life, a badge of loyalty and an image of devotion. He asked me to marry him. I accepted.

My father's habitual dullness sparked into angry life when I broached the subject of marriage. Was it not to avoid this very calamity that I had been banished to Edinburgh? He begged, instructed and even threatened that I should reconsider. So quitting the Misses MacRaes' roof for the last time, I came home to reconsider. But my original conclusion was unmoved. James McLehose was the one I would marry.

It is true that James was only a law agent, yet his family were respectable and with application he would surely progress. So it was not an issue of social position that drove my father's opposition. That I was too young was his constant theme, while all around me girls were marrying at sixteen, seventeen and eighteen. I was seventeen and maturely grown. I believe that my poor parent was animated by fear. Had marriage and childbearing not led to the death of his beloved spouse, and then of our dear Margaret? Would I also be subsumed in the grim shadow? As I said, my father was no Calvinist yet he began now to forebode some fateful predestination. I myself have not dealt in these dark tenets.

My will was adamantine and soon I stood beside my James, he two heads taller and elegant in black, as we made our vows and joined hands together. My father looked on helplessly, bent by the force of events. Should I have heeded his fears, or was this path of sorrows my true vocation? Only time, or perhaps somewhere beyond time, will reveal to us the whole circumstances of our heart's inner motions.

What I have now to relate is painful in the extreme. Yet I cannot pass it over while remaining true to myself and to you. I trust entirely to your delicacy and discretion, since I wish to look this matter in the eye, or at least through the eyes of a caring and sympathetic friend. Many have heard a part of this story but few the whole, and if we are to correspond as between equals then I must count you in that select number. Forgive me, Sylvander, if anything in my account offends or repulses. I have already appointed you the inmost guardian of my honour, and if I have any fault it is that when I give, I give all without restraint.

The first months of married life are strange to both parties. However closely these two lives have moved, living together all of a sudden in the same cramped rooms comes as a surprise. I have already described James as shy and constrained, and I felt that in those first weeks he was only gradually becoming used to my presence. He was diffident yet considerate. I felt no qualms about the future of our union. Our first experiences of love were clumsy but comforting.

I must confess that my housekeeping may not have been of the highest standard. The contribution of the Misses MacRae to domestic economy was limited to the correct manner of pouring tea or distributing cups. It was not therefore surprising that on occasion my young husband stayed later at some tavern to enjoy a solitary supper. At such times I was glad of my own company or the opportunity to visit friends.

However, this was to become the cause of a first rupture in my so far unbroken calm. I had been calling on some friends in the Trongate, and in the process of leaving was daffing with a couple of my old set at the stair-foot. Suddenly James appeared, striding along the road. On seeing us he came to an abrupt halt. A dark shadow crossed his features. Without a word of greeting or polite notice he broke into the circle, took me rudely by the arm, wheeled me out and hurried me homeward. I remonstrated with him but was ignored. On entering the house he launched into a tirade of abuse and blame. I remained silent, as if wary that any response on my part might lead to blows.

For two days I was in a state of paralysed fear. Nothing further was said. Then, as suddenly as the storm had appeared, it evaporated; the black cloud cleared from James's brow and I breathed more easily.

I remember this nightmare episode as if it had occurred yesterday. Yet at the time I smoothed it over as an inexplicable outburst that had to be left to one side so that life could proceed as before. At this time I made the happy discovery that I was expecting a baby. James was delighted. All his kindness was renewed and I forgave and even forgot, cocooned in the prospect of motherhood.

Alas it was not to be. My first bairn, a little boy, was

stillborn, and I had to be nursed gently back to health. My father's old maid Bella came to look after me, though I was aware of James on the edge of things, helping where possible but withdrawing to his own devices. Total rest was meat and drink to my exhausted body and soul.

Gradually I picked up again where I had left off. Was there a change in my husband's attitude to me, a subtle shift of mood? I cannot definitely say the change was not in me. Yet something felt different. There was a constant watchfulness in his demeanour. We went on much as before but his absences from home increased. Did he blame me in an obscure way for the loss of our baby?

Soon in God's providence I was once again expecting a child. But this time there was no delight or tender solicitude from my husband. So one evening after supper I asked James if anything was troubling him or if I had displeased him in any way. This produced a second violent outburst. He accused me of neglecting our house in favour of flippant society. I was not prepared to accept this charge passively, since apart from visiting at the Saltmarket, my lonely days were bereft of society, flippant or otherwise.

I might have saved my breath. This attempt at justification only redoubled his fury. A spate of denigration combined with sexual innuendo overwhelmed my feeble defences. My family had always looked down on him, he said. From the beginning I had maintained a secret superiority. Did I think he was a fool, unable to detect the smug mockery that lay behind my words and actions? However submissive my posture at home, my heart was disobedient and wilfully contriving his humiliation.

I was so shocked, I was incapable of intelligent reply. I broke down in tears. Slamming the door behind him, he left me to my own devices.

That was the beginning of our married war. It lasted through two pregnancies and the births of my two lovely sons. At times the illusion of normal life spread over our little house and family. But the darkness always resurfaced. James would stay out late and then lie in bed, refusing company or nourishment. The husband whom I had pledged to love, honour and obey became for me a lord of doubleness, one day cheerful and kind, the next spitting blame and recrimination. The very sight of me at his bedside could provoke a spasm of disgust and hate.

I realised that the black moods were linked to James' absences from home, a slurring of speech and the odours of the tavern. Yet to this day I believe drink was a symptom and not the cause of his malaise. He was trying to dampen his devils, not to raise them. They stared dully and malevolently from his eyes, daring my displeasure.

James seemed able to control his moods in the presence of others. We would visit his widowed mother or my father, and sometimes relatives would come to us after our first boy was safely born. On these days he would be genial and polite, even though I could see the huge effort of self-control this cost him. When our visitors had gone, he would find fault with my hospitality or bearing or conversation, whipping himself up till vent could be given to his suppressed anger and hatred.

I should not have argued back but I did. I was furious at his hypocritical determination to put me in the wrong and force my abject submission. What could I do but defend the little space of life still left to me and my child? It was as if his morbid shame needed to tear down my virtuous image and put a reflection of his own tormented self in its place. But when I fought back James relished my resistance, crushing me with contempt and an icy control more terrifying than his rages.

It was that presumption of moral and intellectual superiority, his threat to expose my supposed wrongdoing, that led me gradually to confide in others, particularly close female friends. By this time, apart from my father, I was jealously denied any male company. Yet by nature, Sylvander, I am an Amelia. I would rather tolerate the wandering of a Booth than cast a husband from my door. But I have not the spaniel in my being to suffer public humiliation, or allow who knows what sinister imputations on my reputation and character. It was too much. I spoke to my father of separation. He urged caution.

My waist was thickening with a new child. I feared for the health of this baby and insisted on withdrawal from those hated rooms at Townhead, in which the sordid drama of these last three years had been endured. Submission was no longer bearable.

Perceiving my husband's disposition and temper to be so discordant as to permanently banish any hope of happiness, I made my plans. Our disagreements had risen to such a pitch that I feared for my safety. With the support of my remaining friends a separation finally took place and in December 1780 I returned to my family home.

For a moment an old life flickered and we lived like a family again and I was numb to outside society as I awaited the birth of my new baby. Then a lovely William was added to my Andrew. Bella took everything in hand, and even my mother's shade seemed to summon up a pale smile.

We had heard little from my husband since the separation, but now his duplicitous talent was put grandly on display. Acting the aggrieved parent, he commanded that Andrew and even the babe at my breast be removed to his mother's house for their proper upbringing. He had the power of law on his side and well he knew it. Simultaneously, he wrote begging me to return to our home and restore his happiness through the reunion of our family. Everything he did and said pretended sanctity while cruelly conniving to sunder a mother from her newborn infant. Worst of all, he believed in his own deceit. The sanctimonious prig was armoured against any dunt of self-reproach, while the drunk veered from depression to violent denunciation and back. This was – no, is – the husband to whom I have pledged myself body and soul till death.

Fortunately his mother, who was a kindly soul, held no grudge against me. She quietly ensured access to her house so that my bond with the two little ones was strained but not broken. She hoped always for the best from her son, only to have her expectations dashed. I was able to see at first hand that for James the maternal relation, like that of marriage, was as much honoured in the breach as the observance.

These strange weeks stretched into months and then into a year. My only consolation was the rediscovery of poetry. I read as I had never read before, mapping out the territories of natural beauty, of sentiment, of tender regret. My feelings were stretched taut and tuned like a Grecian lyre. Author after author was consumed in verse and prose: Thomson, Shenstone, Cowper, Richardson, Fielding, Sterne and many more of your own tutors. These were the makers of my landscape, the enclosures of my soul, and I began to relieve my pent-up feelings by composing my own fragments of verse.

It was at this period that my thoughts turned back to Edinburgh. Was it not the literary town, the centre of enlightenment, where I might recover my inner poise and explore the universes of feeling and thought? Perhaps this view of Edinburgh was coloured by my early experience of romance. Was it wrong to imagine a place more refined than Glasgow's frank mercantile commerce – somewhere beckoning from my precious memories towards the future?

Did Edinburgh, Sylvander, live up to my expectations? Perhaps you can still help me solve that puzzle.

Whatever my perceptions, harsh circumstance took a sudden hold on my dreams. My father, who had for some months been ailing and unable to fulfil his duties, suddenly died. It was as if he had surrendered unintentionally and without warning to the unequal struggle of existence. We buried him in the Ramshorn kirkyard amidst an abundant congregation of colleagues and well wishers. I think now that I did not truly value his constancy and steadfastness; then I felt – and still feel – his absence keenly.

It quickly became apparent that my dear father's illness and his benevolence over so many years had left him bereft of capital, material capital at least. After settlement of his debts there was barely fifty pounds of ready money but still in his possession were two tenement dwellings in the Saltmarket besides our own house, and sale of these secured me a meagre annuity of twenty pounds.

Meanwhile Mr McLehose had dispatched to London in search of better fortune. His rare letters home revolved around emigration to Jamaica. Prosperity was apparently assured in that colony, and he pressed his desire to be reunited with his 'beloved' wife and children. In reality not a penny trickled through to either party. Instead, reports of drunken debauch, gaming debts and despairing dissolution were relayed to Glasgow by reliable witnesses. Finally the McLehose family realised the hopelessness of their case and urged me to reclaim the care of my two dear sons.

Glasgow was still a close-knit town. My father's friends became assiduous in my cause: the College of Surgeons, and then the lawyers also, voted me a pension, in recognition of my cruel desertion by the broken reed which should have been my principal stay. My thoughts flew to Edinburgh and the chance of a new beginning, with my little ones brought back under their mother's wing.

It was a cold, wet day in early June 1782 when I stepped off the Glasgow coach. Imagine my reflections as I remembered that other journey to Edinburgh, the company I kept and the illusions I had harboured. Now I was entirely alone, standing with my bags outside the White Hart Inn and all the bustle of the Grassmarket indifferent around me. I started the climb up West Bow, the wind against me, blowing icy rain into my face. I felt defeated, spurned and painfully solitary. So despite my slender means I hailed a sedan chair at St Giles, and leaving my baggage in a porter's cart I was carried to my cousin William's apartments on the north side of the High Street.

I should have explained that of all our relations it was the family of Uncle William Craig, my father's minister brother, who had stood with me through my troubles and afforded me every practical assistance. My older cousin, lawyer William, welcomed me into his handsome, book-lined study, and listened intently as I poured out my anxieties and hopes. So unaccustomed had I become to a sympathetic ear, that at points I was close to tears. William promised to help me find an apartment and to support my efforts to bring my sons to join me.

Perhaps he felt a little awkward sheltering me in his bachelor rooms; within a week he had settled me in a little apartment on the south side of Auld Reikie, at General's Entry, off the Potterrow. And this is still the neuk in which I have built my cosy bield. George Square is just round the corner, with the town-houses of the Duchess of Gordon and other notables.

I am very grateful to dear William for his tactful assistance, but also because as a lawyer and litterateur he had entry to all the best circles of Edinburgh society. Nonetheless I was determined to make my own way and soon gathered round me a small group of friends – Miss Nimmo, as you know, Miss Peacock, James Gray the schoolmaster and his lovely wife Mary, Dr Blacklock the blind poet and others whose tastes coincide with my own.

Soon I was in my element, hosting intimate literary soirées and handing round delicate china cups. And now I have the friendship of an incomparable poetic talent. Do I sound trivial or fashionable, Sylvander? Truly I find consolation in the conversation of my equals. When solitary, I brood over my books and am strengthened. I felt more alive again in Edinburgh than for many years past.

Meanwhile news reached Glasgow of my husband's departure for Jamaica. It transpired that he had left under a cloud of temporary imprisonment due to debt. He continued to importune me with hectoring letters which, incredibly, appealed to my conscience and finer feelings, on which he had trampled so mercilessly: 'Early this morning I leave this country for ever and therefore wish to pass some short time with you. Upon my word of honour, my dearest Nancy, it is the last night you will ever have an opportunity of seeing me in this world.' You see, I have these passages by heart.

The proposed meeting did not take place. My friends advised against seeing him and I declined an interview.

However, James now finally released the children into my arms. For all his protestations to the contrary, he found the boys an encumbrance. He wrote implying that the little ones' plight lay at my door, urging me to return from Edinburgh, the sooner the better, to take 'these enduring pledges of our once happier days' under my protection. None of his friends would have anything to do with them.

His final letter, written on embarkation, bade me farewell with the assurance that, 'For my part, I am willing to forget what is past, neither do I require an apology from you.' I have this letter still, stained with tears of rage. I lost no time in bringing Andrew and William to Potterrow. And despite the infant's indifferent health, the boys settled into our small home with all the happy resilience of children.

If I have merit in anything, Sylvander, it is in my unfailing tenderness to my offspring. A worldly woman once told me in company that she was surprised by my love for them, considering what kind of a father they had. I replied that I could do no other than love my boys, and that the misfortune of such a father doubly endeared them to my heart. They are innocent; they depend on me; what higher claim can there be on my humanity? While I live, my fondest attention shall be theirs.

There is great virtue in friendship. It is medicine for the soul and food for the mind, even when the dearest relations in life have been snatched away. Let us cast every kind of feeling, Sylvander, into the allowed bond of friendship. No malignant demon, as you suppose, was permitted to fill my cup with sorrow, but the wisdom of a tender Father who foresaw that I needed chastisement before I could be brought to myself.

My dear friend, religion converts our heaviest misfortunes into blessings. I feel it to be so. Those passions naturally too violent for my peace have been broken and moderated by adversity. And if even that has been unable to conquer my vivacity, to what lengths might I have gone had I glided along in undisturbed prosperity! Would I have forgotten our ultimate destination and fixed my happiness on these fleeting shadows below? My heart was formed for love and I desire to devote it to Him who is the source of love.

These convictions are encouraged in me by an especial friend and adviser, John Kemp, minister of the Tolbooth Church. How I wish you might meet him, Sylvander. His wise counsel, his manly blend of reason and religion, guides me in the right paths. Mr Kemp is father confessor to my wounded, orphaned soul. Because of his devotion I am never without a confiding ear.

For many years I have sought for a male friend endowed with sentiments like yours, one who could regard me with tenderness unmixed with selfish desire, who could be my companion and protector, who would die sooner than injure me. I sought but I sought in vain. Heaven has, I hope, sent me this blessing now.

I have been puzzling my brain about the fair one whose loss has wounded your heart. At first I thought it must be your Jean, but I don't know if she possesses your deepest most faithful friendship. I cannot understand that bonnie lassie: her refusal after such proofs of love proves her to be either an angel or a dolt.

I beg pardon for reading between the lines of your life, but you have thrown out many hints and suggestions in your poetry. I do not know all the circumstances and am therefore no judge. I admire your continued fondness even after enjoyment – few of your sex have souls in such cases. I take this to be the test of true love; mere desire is all that most people are susceptible of, and that is soon sated.

You told me you never met with a woman able to love as ardently as yourself. I believe it and would advise you never to tie yourself with uxorious bonds till you meet such a one. You will find many who canna and some who mauna, but to be joined to one of either description would make you miserable. I think you had best resolve against wedlock, for unless a woman were qualified for companion, friend and mistress, she would not do for you. The last may gain possession but only the other two can keep hold.

I have read the packet you sent me, twice, with close attention. Some parts beguile me to tears. With Desdemona, I felt 'twas pitiful, 'twas wondrous pitiful. When I reached the bit about your youthful struggles, I burst out in open sobs. It was that delightful flooding of the heart which arises from a combination of the keenest sympathies with the most pleasurable sensations. Nothing is so binding to a generous mind as to have so much confidence placed in it. You seem to be perfectly acquainted with that side of my nature.

One thing alone hurt me, though I regretted many. It was your avowal of being an enemy to Calvinism. I guessed it was so but the confirmation in your own personal testimony gave me a shock I could only have felt for someone who concerned me deeply. You know that I am a strict Calvinist, excepting those dark doctrines to which I referred. Like many others, you are prejudiced, either by never having examined the creed with candour and impartiality, or from having met with weak and hypocritical disciples who do not understand these tenets or use them as a cloak for knavery. Both types abound and I should not be surprised by their effect on your own enlightened understanding.

Your favourite discourse is the 'religion of the bosom'. Did you imagine I meant any other? Poor would be that religion whose seat is merely the brain. I found all my hopes of pardon and acceptance with Heaven upon Christ's atonement, whereas you base all on a good life. If anything we could do had been able to make good the violation of God's moral law, where was the need – and I speak with reverence – of such an astonishing sacrifice? It is pride, my friend, that prevents us from embracing Jesus: we scorn to be indebted to God's only Son and would be our own saviours. Yet He, and He alone, is the foundation of our hopes, to some a stumbling block, to others foolishness, but to those who believe the wisdom of God and the power of Love.

If my head did not ache I would continue on this subject, but the story of my life has advanced to this present time. And besides, I hate controversial religion. But is my plea for mercy not religion of the bosom.

My God, Sylvander, why am I so anxious to have you embrace the Gospel in all its fullness? I dare not look too deep for an answer. Let your own heart provide one.

All my esteem and benevolence are at your disposal,

Yours ever, CLARINDA.

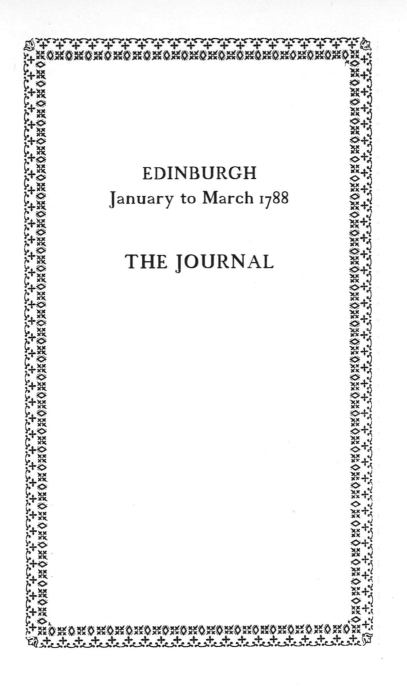

EDINBURGH
January to March 1788

THE JOURNAL

HAVE SENT MY life in sheets to Clarinda. I had intended to place it in her hands but changed my mind at the last. Nancy is a different prospect in the flesh, quite different from my previous brief impression in company. She was of course *en pleine toilette,* with abundant curls piled high, curbed only by a blue silk ribbon – a graceful spray of lace behind. The hair is blonde, deep, fair to the roots. Cheeks and lips delightfully full, eyes alight beneath lush curving lashes. A dainty dish to tempt any gourmand; yet she was tense, and pleading a headache.

We were *enfin à deux.* Very proper yet confidential, old friends and correspondents. She steered the conversation in literary directions, while my remarks were personal, yet discreet. How could we come to know each other better, now that the Rubicon of meeting had been crossed? I was glad to remember my epistle to Dr Moore and promised to send her a copy: 'How remiss not to have forwarded it before.' She promised to consider a reply, but in the meantime gave me more verses. I expressed due appreciation. We were genial, at ease grazing on safe pastures, and parted promising to write soon. No pressure or presumption on either side.

I was meditating another meeting, and how to suggest it, my letter scarce begun, when a note arrived from – Miss Nimmo's brother, the Excise Officer. It was a reply to mine of some days since, saying he is now ready to conduct my formal interview. So I hastened to obey, gathering up my best coat, my crutch, and my certificate of bachelorhood. No man ever appeared better qualified.

Nimmo was correct yet friendly. We shall see what comes of it, if anything. When he signs my examination, I shall write to Graham of Fintry. That gentleman is my best remaining hope of some preferment beyond the plough.

Tired after all this unwonted exertion, I stayed in to cultivate anew my best confidante. These pages are needed more than ever. The next few weeks may prove decisive in this poor wandering fellow's earthly pilgrimage.

Up with the lark; breakfast in the kitchen accompanied by Betty's ministrations. Nimmo's signed examination came round – wholly favourable. Do I owe this to the good sister Nimmo or simply to plain honesty? Wrote immediately to Fintry. When Lear asks Kent why he wishes to be in his service he answers 'because you have that in your face I could like to call master'. This is the substance of my appeal: I solicit his patronage to be admitted an Officer of Excise.

I have the papers in due order; I have no wife (two children living, but not reckoned by His Majesty's Customs), propriety of conduct as a man, and fidelity to duty. Above all, this may be my only chance of a sufficiency outwith that miserable struggle for bread, which would have sent my father into the maws of imprisonment had death not swallowed him first. I am your most humble servant.

Hobbled round to Johnny Dowie's to toast unexpected prospects of good fortune, and renew my acquaintance with the town.

Long epistle this morning from Nancy on her favoured topic – religion. Put to one side for later consideration. Instead hobbled, nay, hopped, round to Creech.

'Why, Mr Burns, what an unexpected pleasure.'

'I am much improved.'

'So I see with my own eyes. We have business to settle, Mr Burns, author's affairs.'

'Yes, and that is why—'

'So come ben, come ben, my dear fellow, Edinburgh's *illuminati* are gathered here in the shop. Come through and give us the time of day.'

No change in that quarter. But at least the old privateer has sighted the brig Burns on his horizon. Full sail ahead, boarding party ahoy.

I looked in on Johnson. He is desperate to conclude the second volume – wife and children at wits end and so forth. I pledged it my full attention.

Dined out with Willie and Bob, freemen to a man. They received me back with open arms, long lost brothers reunited in communion of wit and the bottle.

Alas, this proved poor preparation for my theological disquisition, but I screwed myself manfully to the task.

Our Author and Preserver, Clarinda, knows our frailty and we respond with reverence and awe by native impulse. He is not willing that any should perish but that all should come to eternal life. This is the religion of benevolence and of everlasting joy. The mean-spirited or uncharitable exclude themselves requiring no banishment to outer darkness since the dark is already in them. But to guide us the Creator has made Jesus Christ, whose relation to Him we cannot comprehend, though we know he is a light to our path.

That, I believe, is sincerely put, but a harmless falsehood may also be apt. Clarinda's letter announces her presence in St James Square at two o'clock this afternoon when I was otherwise engaged. 'I watched at the window for you but was disappointed.'

Enough – timorous criticisms are no concern of mine.

I have dashed off the letter and sealed it. 'Tis now the witching time, and whatever is out of joint is the fault of spells and enchantments. She will be fast asleep. I kiss the messenger, warm wax moulded by my breathing lips. May good angels attend and guard you as my good wishes.

> Beauty which whether waking or asleep
> Shot forth peculiar graces.

Good night, Clarinda, and may God grant my restless soul peace tonight. Let me have a larger share of dull cart-horse plodding home, native, dumb, unconscious bliss.

Soberly sat down to reckon my day's account. Uncomfortable night followed by restless day. Little morning left to me, but glanced at Johnson's promised selection, then went out instead of settling to my task.

I intended to nod at Creech, justifying this as a pecuniary measure, albeit one without return. However, met Nicol on the road, apparently playing truant from his pupils, so we repaired to the Canongate to evade untimely sightings.

What a strange tormented spirit Nicol is, always in revolt. Resentment against his headmaster, Adam, a harmless scholar, boils over. Adam's attempt to govern, reasonable enough in the circumstances, stifles Nicol's very breath, aggravates his inner soul. He is like Milton's Satan, but with smouldering fire gnawing at his vitals. Prometheus or Satan?

Yet Nicol is frank and free – as I learned to my cost on our summer tour. Neither Reverend nor Duchess is spared his satiric scorn or proud resentment. Even at Atholl

Castle I had to withdraw in order to accommodate his self-imposed exclusion. Nicol is no Bob Ainslie, trimming and tacking to the company.

Amidst other talk, Nicol referred to the Deacon and told me outright that this denizen of Auld Reikie's darker deeps is none other than William Brodie, Deacon of the Guilds and prominent citizen of our capital town. How could he live in such duplicity and escape detection? Because, according to Nicol, Edinburgh is a festering corpse in which worms twist and cavort, hidden even to their own kind. It suits many to mix the legal and the clandestine. My appetite was whetted.

I drank little after last night's convivial turn, nursing a queasy gut, but William drank steadily. I launched him homewards, then veered off into Canongate kirkyard to inspect my headstone to poor Fergusson – is he not living and dying proof of Nicol's bitter philosophy? The Muse of Scotia's ancient tongue would have lain unremarked and unremembered in the same mooly earth that covers murdered Darnley and all this shipwrecked host of priests, merchants and makars. Perhaps that is the fate of poets: neglected when alive and only reluctantly recalled when dead. At the last, Fergusson was confined to the madhouse, unable to pay even a doctor's bill, far less his funeral expenses. The spectres entered his brain and posssesed his wracked and wasted body, till the bones rubbed through his raw skin and the fevered light in his eyes went out. Is that what Edinburgh holds for me?

Returned home to find a package from Clarinda. It is the story of her life up till this point, and needs deliberate reading. I shall take it to bed. She wants to meet me on Friday, even though one of her boys has been ill. She wonders that I can write at all after sitting two or three hours over a bottle with indifferent company. No wonder I should turn at last to a congenial friend who can relish most things with me, except port.

I sense that Clarinda herself was once heart and soul of the party, but now her spirits are pruned and restrained from merriment. Everything in her situation makes prudence necessary. The key to these allusions lies in the bulky packet, a riposte to my autobiographical account. Tomorrow.

Tomorrow she will walk again in St James Square, allowing the poet a distant view.

Keep a good heart, Sylvander, the eternity of your lone sufferings will be ended soon. By what means though, madam, by whose gentle ministrations? Compose yourself to rest. Sweet sleep attend us both, lest we toss and turn on the unhavened, unshriven sea.

Disturbed night. Trust this is not an early sign of old troubles. I read Clarinda's *Life* with sympathy and admiration. She is no plaything but a woman of spirit and resource – a true friend for the poet and perhaps an unequalled lover. As she herself describes it, one who combines the companion, the friend and the mistress.

I never met with a woman like this before, with one honoured exception. Her name is indelibly written in my heart's core, and not for a second would I allow selfish gratification to stain or tarnish her image. Clarinda has been puzzling her brain about who that one might be. Peggy Chalmers is worthy of a place in the same bosom, the same embrace, as my Clarinda. That is the highest compliment I can pay to each.

Had a strange dream last night in the twilight betwixt

sleep and waking. A great golden eagle wheeled and swooped in the sunlit sky. Nestling in a bush was a white breasted turtle dove. I looked on transfixed as the talons descended, then at the last reached out my hand. The warm-hearted bosom throbbed in my cupped palm and I awoke.

Taking another batch of songs up to Johnson. The Muse was moved by my gleaning of Highland airs. Might tender emotion still revive the poet?

Musing on the roaring ocean
Which divides my love and me,
Wearying heaven in warm devotion
For her weal where'er she be
Hope and Fear's alternate billow
Yielding late to nature's law
Whispering spirits round my pillow
Talk of her that's far awa.

Will Johnson notice this new inspiration? Will Clarinda?

Watched out for my fair one promenading in the Square, the boys at her side. But Clarinda does not look to the right storey for a poet's lodging – 'where speculation roosted near the sky'.

Met up with Bob and Willie. Bit by bit all the old Crochallan fellowship came ben till there was a full rattlin roarin night. Toasts and songs intertwined so I gave out some of my new verses, turning bardic on the instant.

Landlady count the lawin
The day is near the dawin
Ye're aa blind drunk bots
And I'm jolly fou.

I'll set it with a couple more verses to 'Hey Tutti Tati', with a chorus it will please the general. But not the poor poet wha is nae fou but hertsair. What has Edinburgh left for me? German Geordie's Excise, and her fair head on a distant pillow.

> Gentle night do thou befriend me
> Downy sleep the curtain draw
> Spirits kind again attend me.

Unable to rise this morning. Blood pounding, fiery bands of pain tight around head and chest. I tried to lie still and calm but a cold sweat of fear gathered on my brow. Thank God for Betty and her soothing cloot. She brought up some foul concoction that immediately eased the rack.

I lay drained of strength as if my night had been spent in combat rather than slumber. But my mind raced ahead down well-worn paths. What if I could not recover my dues from Creech? What if Miller could wait no longer for an answer about his farm? If Mossgiel fails? If my Excise Commission is spurned like my Dundas poem? My mother, Gilbert, and the surviving bairns turned onto the road or in a debtors' jail? What would happen to Jean and her unborn babe? I might die here and join Fergusson in the unforgiving clay.

There at least I would know peace.

Terror threatened to drive me up and out into the open air, but my limbs were dead to feeling. Gradually my devils subsided. I may have dozed. By lunchtime I was able to take some gruel; the crisis had passed. Even in this kind house, some will ascribe my perturbation to the effects of wine. But yesterday, despite convivial company,

I drank barely a bottle across the full extent. Something else undermines my constitution, and always has since I followed the plough.

Three letters arrived before supper.

The Excise acknowledging my application, courteous yet non-committal. Miller, genial but urging a final visit to decide on Ellisland. And Clarinda.

What did I say or do to draw this frank rebuttal? What I said in my last letter only the gods of fuddling sociability can answer. My good star was partly on the horizon, but then this evil planet which has shed its baleful rays on my head most of my life came to its zenith. And I blabbed something in spite of myself. How I could curse circumstances and the coarse ties of human law which bar the happiness that love and honour otherwise warrant. God spare me any more hairbreadth escapes.

My 'ravings' and 'ambiguous remarks' Clarinda repudiates with a direct warning: take care lest virtue demands even friendship as a sacrifice. Why accuse human law when she can gain nothing from its breach? At present her children are provided for; in the other case she becomes dependent on the bounty of a friend.

This is an open hint of Cousin Craig's support, kind in substantials but without feelings of romance. Is that really how she sees his solicitudes? Yet who would protect her in the face of worldly condemnation and derision? Would a Sylvander – son of whim and fancy – have the courage? And would not ruin be the consequence? Would a former lover speak for Mrs McLehose? But how could she accept one who was not dearer to her than all the world? So run Clarinda's own hectic fears.

And her conclusion? Clarinda must commit all into the hands of God since she has no power to dispose of herself. So the wheel turns irrevocably back to divinity. Let us discourse, Sylvander, on the religion of the bosom. To hell with that, lay hands instead on the bare-breasted idols of the goddess.

But see, she anticipated my every thought. She knows and feels. She figures me in a state of celibacy, while wishing me happily married since I cannot thrive without a tender attachment. She screws me to the maddening pinpoint of desire, and then denies that very attachment. Farewell, Sylvander, be wise, be prudent, be happy? I appeal before the throne of love, is this benevolence or witchery?

Tomorrow I will have this out with her or break off for good. Now I am fit for nothing but Betty's warm milk and sops.

Today I believe the game became deadly serious. Nancy McLehose has entered my soul and I must record events with special care since the clues or hopes of my future happiness have been sown in these hours. It feels as if I have lived three days since I rose, recovered and resolute.

First I dashed off a strong reply to Clarinda's letter. *Thoughts on religion are to be welcomed but let us at all costs avoid controversial divinity. Where we fondly love we should not reproach. As Bolingbroke said to Swift, 'Adieu, my dear Swift, with all thy faults I love thee entirely: make an effort to love me with all mine'. A glorious sentiment without which there can be no true friendship.*

This went off by messenger before eleven, with the promise that by the middle of the coming week I would be able to walk to Potterrow. Before the hour, a tearstained epistle flew back, the messenger held till she could compose her reply. She could not bear the grief of offending me. Everything she wrote had been bathed in affection and esteem, but for whatever thought or word had inflicted hurt she begged forgiveness. Had her freedom of expression, meant in sincere friendship, been unpardonable? Then, heaven help her, she would accept my sentence of dismissal.

This was overwrought, yet opened up the springs of feeling. Keeping the messenger again, I responded immediately. Offend me, my dearest angel, you cannot offend; you never offended me. If you had ever given me the least shadow of offence, so pardon me, my God, as I forgive without reservation or constraint.

I was expecting Nicol for tea, or else I would have taken a chair then and there. Instead I sent my letter as foretaste and pledge of my arrival at eight o'clock. As it was I became unsettled and impatient. Nicol did his best to damp my fires with scathing asides but I was deaf to his mordant observations. Finally my leg was bent into the sedan and I was on my way to General's Entry, jogged along by the sure footfall of the cadies.

My welcome was warm and tearful, her face newly cleansed. Emotion bubbled near the surface. The boys were settled in the backroom, Clarinda drew me to the fireside. The discourse of our letters passed into conversation without any artificial barrier. Such was the benevolent effect of the day's contrary passages.

As we smoothed out the tangles and filled in the gaps of understanding, I took her hand across the hearthside. We seemed made to share our innermost thoughts. I moved my seat closer to hers. Then the floodgates burst. The loneliness and cruelty of her situation welled up beyond restraint. To have such capacity for love and be denied outlet. Every natural tie hemmed in or broken by death and narrow obligation. Dependence on the charity of those who could snuff out her fragile independence at will. Subjugation to convention and the mores of drawing rooms to which her own access was severely limited.

These were denials and humiliations written on my own soul from birth, and my heart overflowed in sympathy. Her head lay gently on my shoulder. I put my arm around her till the sobs and tears subsided into soulful peace.

After the storm blows out its passions, profound calm. How long we sat there. I inhaled her yielding softness through every pore. I rested in her ample warmth, the rise and fall of neck, shoulder, breast. But I dared not move lest I dispelled the charm which had beguiled us with this moment. Eventually, as if by unspoken mutual consent, we drew apart to let the silence settle between us. What more to say? We had shared all by intuition. The hours had flown. The chair was called, our evening ended. The curtain closes on reconciliation of the lovers, harmony of the spheres. For now at least.

I came straight home reluctant to mar the spell, yet eager to recall the day in all its fullness. For once I am content to surrender all into the hands of a loving God. Is this what stern believers call regeneration, to be born again? If so, then Saul has been changed to Paul. I have been called from the old Adam to a new creation.

Slept deeply. Woke still buoyed by the yesterday evening's transport of souls.

Limped round to Miers and arranged to have Clarinda's profile done. Once the silhouette is obtained from the life, he can make a card, locket or a breastpin. From the studio I sent round one of mine with a card, asking her to sit for

Miers so that we could make a true exchange.

Called in at Johnson's to find work proceeding merrily for Volume Two. Nothing further is needed from me except to proof the sheets when they are ready.

Returned home to find a want of communication from Potterrow. Dozed placidly in the content of my newfound highmindedness.

Nicol called in – why so suddenly assiduous? – but I refused his company in the name of an aching leg. The pain was true but the place is my heart and not my limb.

Supper came and went still with no letter. Then a messenger was announced and my spirits danced. It was some cursed versifier offering me his first effusions: prose run mad without a syllable of poetry.

Eventually I sat down and wrote another missive to Clarinda, asking to meet again before I had to leave Edinburgh – Saturday or sooner if at all possible. Seasoned it with some apt quotations.

I like to have quotations suitable to every occasion; they give one's ideas so pat and save the bother of finding a correct expression for all one's feelings. One of the few compensations of poetic gifts is this ability to render sorrows, joys and loves in a ready compact form. A small kindness that the Muse can bestow.

Thou source of all my bliss and all my woe
Who found me poor at first, and keeps me so

What in all damnation is the matter with Clarinda? Morning brings neither news nor respite. Very lackadaisical but pulled myself up to face the day.

Wrote first to Miller assuring him of an early visit to settle the farm business. No sooner penned, than I was driven out to enquire from Nimmo about the Commission. He has heard nothing yet from his superiors but expects they will write directly to the applicant, by which he means poor benighted me – an applicant!

Paid a few social calls leaving copies of my Elegy wherever I felt it proper. Who knows which of these Edinburgh worthies knows someone on the Excise Board.

Returned to a late bowl of soup and stretched out my leg on a cushion. Clarinda continued dumb – was she in some distress? An unbearable contemplation. I took up her life story and perused it once more.

How unjust it is that this exceptional woman should be shackled to the very man who has failed her so miserably. Is this not a form of slavery? How desperately she craves another mainstay, beyond the crabbed and grudging prop offered by society. I would be the one but as it is I cannot. Even Romeo and Juliet were less blighted in their amours than Sylvander and Clarinda. Perhaps McLehose will die in the Indies – he deserves little better – and my lovely woman will hold freedom in her hands again.

Desultory afternoon, so flicked through the pages of *Amelia*, borrowed on Clarinda's recommendation. They would get on well, Bob and Nancy. Both aspire to be free spirits but have respectability bred in their bones. For all his philandering, Booth is preferred by Clarinda over a brutal yet constant husband, so acutely alive is her sensibility to kindness and unkindness. This is McLehose's education. Brooding as I was on Clarinda's situation, a messenger finally appeared from Potterrow to match my musings.

There are things in this letter I shall treasure to my dying breath: *Few such evenings, Sylvander, fall to the lot of humankind, and few are formed to relish the exquisite pleasure. You saw Clarinda behind the scenes, and I have met few of your sex who understand delicacy in these circumstances. Oh my friend, I wish ardently to maintain your esteem. Our last interview has raised you high in mine.*

This praise unmans me and disowns the lover's part. That our mutual enjoyment did not lead beyond virtue's limits gives Clarinda satisfaction, while still regretting the pain our intimacy might give a friend to whom she is bound by ties of gratitude – so, no more. As if Cousin Craig would be peeping in at a first floor window! In the end it comes down, or up, to Heaven's approval, or at least to misgivings that Heaven does not approve. Even I, it seems, may not approve of what I saw behind the scenes, my glimpses of an uncontrolled sensibility.

Can she not see it is that overflowing generosity, that natural abundance which delights the poet, and that I desire nothing more than its unreserved expression? Why does she wound my feelings by suggesting that our commingling of tender emotion would lessen my opinion of her? *My dear, beloved Clarinda, behind the scenes I saw a bosom glowing with benevolence and honour; a mind ennobled and informed by education, exalted by natural religion; a heart formed for all the glorious meltings of which our universe is capable: friendship, love and pity.* These are the perceptions I must pour out before her feet till I convince her 'tis an immortal soul that I desire and not the relish of carnal intercourse.

Unfortunately, she clogs up her letter with some affront she suffered between sermons at Lady Someone's dull luncheon attended by fourteen dolts. These are the rubs we daily encounter in society; soul-commerce is above such mundane stuff. God desires for each of us the inviolate principles of love and amity, the fruits of true religion, not the oafish and mercenary strictures of convention. How can she believe otherwise of a divine creator? Why be dragged down to the idiot level?

When can we meet again, and how soon must we part, Clarinda? I have lost so much by not knowing you sooner, and fear, fear that our acquaintance is too short to make the lasting impression on your heart that I would wish.

Sleep was now impossible, so I wrestled to engraft my sentiments into a letter which would sear Clarinda's soul, and raise her to complete consciousness of my love.

A brisk, sharp sky after the haar and rains. Prepared further copies of the Dundas screed for circulation to Edinburgh notables – a good day to stretch the gammy leg by calling round in person. I devised a standard cover:

> *I enclose you some verses I made on the loss, I am afraid irreparable loss, our Country sustains on the death of the late Lord President. Little new can be said at the time of day in Elegy but the Tribute of the Muse...*

Self-deprecating and tastefully obsequious, as only the poet can be.

Ambled up to the Luckenbooths to call on Creech and attend his levee. Conceive my surprise when I am hailed as a long-lost brother, and assured my affairs are near to settlement. 'The Edition is selling comfortably, Mr Burns, very comfortably. We must conclude accounts, sir, conclude accounts.' All as if I were the impediment to early conclusion!

Is this the harbinger or another false dawn? I remained

phlegmatic. God knows, I must press home my advantage.

Returned home to an acquiescent letter from Clarinda. My last to her was like a key on her pillow; what might this key unlock? An apology at least for being too satiric, too tart an observer. More importantly, a definite assignation for Friday evening, when she will be at home without maid or children. I am to come to tea if I please; but eight will be an hour less liable to intrusions. Also, come by foot. Sedan chairs attract attention. At some later hour a chair home will escape notice.

As for lasting impressions she issues another warning: watch out lest in the tender department she proves half as much a fool as I. This gives me as much as I could possibly hope, and the promise of more. I feel that my open declaration, raising up the spiritual connection, has undermined the stern walls between us. Such are the fruits of honest passion.

Hastened up to Dowie's to celebrate the day's double tidings. A genial company gathered round me and time flew by with songs and clatter till at some point, I did not mark the hour, a fellow slipped into the gathering and whispered in my ear, 'The Deacon would like to see you.' 'Tonight?' 'Aye, the nicht.' Amenably but without haste I finished my wine, and wishing everyone God speed, slipped out into the dark and followed the summoner down to the Cowgate and the subterranean depths of Hastie's Close.

Your blank page stares at me like an accusation. I am strangely reluctant to set down a narrative of last night's encounter. What if a stranger were to scan these pages without my knowledge? Or is it shame? God damn your leering emptiness.

I devote today to idle leisure; it's not up to me to judge. But I need to tell someone, till I gauge what actually transpired. Suffice to say I followed my Charon to the door in Hastie's Close and was admitted to the underworld. This time there was no dithering. I was ushered directly into the Deacon's presence and seated at his table without ceremony.

I felt like someone called to give account of his conduct, Nothing uttered in an Edinburgh tavern seemed to have passed Brodie by. Why was Satan my hero? I tried to put this in its literary context but my host was impatient with *belles lettres*. Was he himself not suitable for the heroic treatment?

A whisper of political discontent had also reached the Old Town warrens. The Deacon put it to me fair and square, man to man: was he not the summit of social defiance? Did his every action not cock the snoot at Auld Reikie's prevailing powers, and reverse the social order?

I regained a measure of *sangfroid*. 'Nay, Deacon,' says I, 'you feed off their hypocrisy.' Like a carrion craw, I might have added, but forbore the analogy.

His brows narrowed; the black eyes fixed on me. 'I do not depend on them,' he snapped, 'nor ever will.' I did not pursue this argument, since I was more curious as to why he had summoned me. Not, presumably, to discuss Milton's hero.

'My life is little understood,' he continued.

'How can it be otherwise?' I queried.

He then proceeded to recount a version of his autobiography to that time. Doting parents, a High School education, financial plenty guaranteed. Yet none of these privileges had shaped or even touched the inner self. So I surmised, as the Deacon poured his tale into my ear like an apothecary spooning sickly syrup.

From bored youth to gambling, cockfighting and worse, Brodie had by his own account progressed downward in one uninterrupted flow. I may have misunderstood, such was the rapid unvarying tone of his narrative, but I believe he claimed to have three wives, with children to each, distributed across the town. I drank it all in without discerning the underlying purpose.

'So, Mr Burns,' he suddenly interposed, 'how can my story be told?'

What could I suggest?

'My fear,' he continued, 'is that my life might end in obscurity.'

'What if someone threatened to expose you?'

A sneer of venomous contempt passed across the smooth features. 'Who would dare? They fear my revenge. I could drag down so many with me.'

'Yet you desire to be known.'

The expression disappeared as he tried to explain what was unsettling him. 'To be unacknowledged – it would be as if I had never lived.'

I could see that. His next gambit caught me completely off guard.

'But you are in the public eye. You have the power to evoke reputation. Make me famous.'

'To be tried and hung like a common criminal?'

'I defy such petty conventions. In that we are alike,' he insinuated. 'Find an indirection, a mask or fiction through which my achievement can be known. After my death the man and the legend can be reunited.'

'But how...'

'You are the poet, Mr Burns. I will of course pay you handsomely.'

At this, a leather pouch appeared as if by sleight of hand at his sleeve. The Deacon shoved it across the polished surface. 'This is only a down payment. I am not a Creech when it comes to coin.'

My eyes involuntarily followed the bag. What was he commissioning? A gallows chapbook like the Newgate tales? A broadside ballad? An epic of crime?

I got unsteadily to my feet promising to consider his proposal. I did not reach towards the money, much as my fingers itched to scoop up the visible evidence of Brodie's patronage.

'Don't delay too long. Who knows what fortune may force upon us tomorrow.'

'Of course. I will return within the week,' I conceded, looking one last time towards the bag as I edged out of the audience chamber. What did the Deacon's last remark mean? Combined with his normal steely demeanour, this gloomy illogic was unnerving.

I won home without incident but have been unprofitable company since. Morose reflections on this strange proposition. Can the author of 'The Dundas Elegy' pen a life of Deacon Brodie? And in whose disguise? Was he serious or merely probing, taunting my weakness? Something in me says he was genuine, needy even. But my moral instinct revolts against such an influence; to have me in his power.

I could ask advice from Nicol, or Ainslie at a stretch. Yet I am reluctant to acknowledge my connection; he is depending on that shame for my silence. But the commission tempts, fascinates by its very difficulty. Why should I spurn the Deacon's silver when Edinburgh spurns the poet?

I cannot write to order. I would have to embrace

Brodie's experience in my moral being. The conjunction of light and dark, as the hero embarks on a terrible descent into violence and chaos. Poor creatures trapped, cowed and driven to desperate acts of mutual self-destruction. Where is the ascent, the journey out? Surely art must reinforce goodness. The hero re-emerges chastened, returned to human fellowship. Can we abide the darkness and remain human or is there a communion also in the dark? The goodly fellowship of defiance and revolt raises its glass against all civility and law. I have drained that cup myself but not to the dregs of violence, not to deface humanity. Not to extinguish the divine impress on earthly clay, a spark of deity amidst the dirt.

Deaving thoughts drive me out to seek distraction. I must have some lightening solace before my evening at Clarinda's. Shake off the Deacon's dust from my boots, which Betty has handsomely buffed.

Later. Potterrow was very quiet as I slipped unnoticed into the entry after eight o'clock. No occasion for scandal. A gentle tap and Nancy herself admitted me to the cosy parlour. Tea and dainties were set out for my arrival along with a new poem by Clarinda for my delectation.

We chatted about little things, our perceptions of the everyday, the incidents of life, mutual warmth drawing us closer. We became quite merry with each other, as if there was no care in the world to intrude on our relaxed intimacy. Eyes met, then hands pressed to cheeks, a daffing kiss, a casual caress that shivers in the flesh, and suddenly our lips and mouths were pressed together open and nakedly hungry. I drew her onto my knee, and as we kissed my hands roamed gently over back, breast, thigh. Her arm was round my shoulder and desire emboldened, enlarged. Till with a sigh, a yearning reluctance, she withdrew her arm, and placing a hand on my shoulder pushed her body upright and away.

'My dear, my darling, what is it?'

She gave no reply but having rearranged her clothes as if in a trance, and patting her lovely curls in place, Clarinda sat on the other side of the table and poured tea. Then she took up literary converse as if we had just renewed a former acquaintance. I protested with a light-hearted pretence that belied my inner passion. She brushed me off with a clumsy attempt at teasing that lay between us like an unacknowledged slight. Things ground towards an inevitable conclusion – departure. This allowed an exchange of kisses and a cursory embrace which told me what her lips denied. Then I was in the close once more, my visit ended.

I was pledged to pick up a sedan in nearby Nicolson Square. But I desired no chair. Every portion of my frame was screaming out for exercise and release. I began to limp vigorously towards the High Street barely conscious of my disability. My legs knew where I was heading as they turned down College Wynd.

There is a corner in the Cowgate, at the foot of Niddrie Wynd, where three or four taverns conjoin. You can always count on company there, gathered in two or threes outside, and retreating into the darkness of the thoroughfare and its adjoining closes. As I came towards this assembly, I caught sight of a known face. I am sure that it was Clarinda's maid Jenny Clow, but my eyes were hunting for a more familiar figure – Jessie Haws.

Jessie is no street girl but a lively, loving lass, with a gleg eye for the poet. I spotted her in the doorway a few yards up the wynd, and swung her on my arm till her warm body was pressed aganst me in the cold night air. 'The Rhymer is it, an whit's yer game the nicht?' I told her with my lips, and she pulled me in, pushing the door behind her with a foot.

Later. We sat together in the Clartie Tavern. Jessie ate and drank with the same frank enjoyment as had sated my appetite half an hour before. Leaving a present in her pocket, I kissed her goodnight, and walked home through the starry frost at more peace with myself than for months before. So I close this day's deliberations, and go content to my rest. God bless the lassies who confer on man his sweetest hours.

Letters early from home: Gilbert, with a scribbled signature enclosed from mother. The harvest has fetched nothing and they are very low. Can I assist again? God help me, with what? The Kilmarnock money is all but gone and Creech has not yielded a single Scots penny. Nothing is possible without ready coin. My own flesh and blood: to be unable to succour her who gave me life itself.

The shame, the pity, that tyrant cruelty, insolent wealth, holds sway on our inmost relations. The world is become icy in its grasp. That vindictive bastard Armour has put Jean out, six months pregnant, in the January snows. God rot his vitals, his bowels, his withered pintle. Sent immediately by messenger to secure her rooms and shelter till my return. These distresses twisting and tightening in my breast. Lay down in a cold sweat of fear and worry. Fit for nothing all day.

Remembered today that John Ballantine might still have some Kilmarnock money in hand. Wrote Gilbert enclosing a note asking Ballantine to accommodate him with twelve pounds, more if he had it. Sent Creech a frosty keen letter on the necessity for immediate payment.

Started an epistle to Clarinda, but out of sorts and could hardly continue. What a creature is man. A little alarm yesterday, and today such a revolution in my spirits that I am mortal. No philosophy or divinity comes half so close to the mind. I have no courage to brave Heaven, only the ravings of an imaginary hero in Bedlam. I can scarce hold up my head or move my hand to write. At least Clarinda cannot see it; she wears Cupid's mask.

Wrote Mrs Dunlop a long apology for being out of touch, explaining my confinement. I must not lose the interest of my Ayrshire friends, particularly my old benefactress and counsellor.

Deferential appeasing letter from Creech, promising payment tomorrow! Even publishers have their turning points, their thus-far-and-no-furthers. But Creech may have marked my own turning too, or returning. Apart from pressing home the Excise business what has Edinburgh left for me? Am I done with this place and it with me – is that what I truly want?

I believe I can reckon on Clarinda's friendship for life, and that her image belongs in my soul.

Hide it, my heart, within that close disguise
Where mixed with God's, her loved idea lies.

We fear inconstancy and the imperfection of human weakness, yet our connection will defy years of absence and the changes or chances of fortune. Only an honest man and a poet of Romance could promise that, but I declare myself both as friend and lover. If womankind be capable of such things then we are matched by heaven.

Transposed this enthusiastic vein into a letter.

We must meet this Wednesday and not delay till Saturday. Time is short and one further Wednesday may bring on the hated day. Tomorrow evening I will call on Miss Nimmo to make my farewells.

Goodnight, Clarinda, nothing can replace your breathing presence in my arms. God bless.

Woke much refreshed after the alarms of Saturday and Sunday. Ate a hearty breakfast, then wrote confidentially to Peggy, wishing her well for married life and sharing my worries about Jean. She knows how hard Mauchline can be for those on whom fortune has frowned.

I am inclined, by the calm light of a new day, to shrug off my recent love passages as a narrow escape. Clarinda's refusal releases me from any obligation or consequence in the natural way. Can I not be heart whole still – waur fleyed than hurt?

'A hairbreadth scape in the imminent deadly breach,' to quote the Moor, who felt the consequence of loving not wisely but too well.

Peggy will not be fooled. She knows my life presents a serious and a melancholy path. The rest is diversion.

Just as I was sealing this, a note came from Clarinda, cold and crabbed but conceding a Wednesday assignation. Come, stubborn pride, unshrinking resolution, accompany me through this miserable world. My limb is almost sound and I will struggle on.

Went up town to hunt out Nicol. His corroding wit matched my mood and revived my humour.

Return to find no word from Creech despite yesterday's promise. Fool, damned lick-spittling, arse-shitting fool,

fool, fool. God have mercy on me, a poor, alarmed, incautious, duped unfortunate. The sport, the helpless victim of rebellious pride, hypochondria, agonising sensibility, and bedlam passions. Unlucky poet.

Sunk low, when Bob called round and took me out. He seems to be a man of leisure since his taskmasters are locked in some great cause at court.

I described the whole Clarinda imbroglio in some detail, to his evident delight. It appears that Bob knows Cousin Craig, whom he described as pedantical and proper. Which is how I sometimes think of Bob. He has also soaked up a quantity of gossip about Nancy's soul-friend, Kemp. The Tron Kirk minister is, it seems, famed for his confiding consultations with female parishioners. From the moment I heard the name of Kemp on her lips I felt instinctively the slimy motion of a snake.

Of course Bob is agog to meet Nancy. Her situation fascinated his curiosity, but I believe his appetite is also whetted by the ambivalence, as he views it, of her behaviour – moral to excess, yet courting danger. He wants an introduction and I will contrive it, while emphasising discretion. When I am away, he may prove an assiduous friend and useful protector to the abandoned.

Finally shaking him off, I returned to St James Square just in time to leave again for Potterrow.

I did not stand on ceremony and she gave herself over to my embrace. We indulged an hour in tender caresses and endearments till her ardour waned. She moved no further than Saturday but I did not press my suit, to her relief or disappointment it was hard to gauge. Some desultory conversation followed about my farewell to Miss Nimmo,

Johnson's next volume and so forth.

As I rose to leave she came to me and for the first time took me in her arms, swearing I was closest to her heart of all living beings. Every contour of her body was pressed to mine, but only because she was sure of my departure. Her boys were sleeping soundly in their beds. Uncertainly, I sought her lips. She broke away with a muffled sob, and I left stumbling in the darkness of the entry.

I came straight home to record the episode, unsure who to blame for this game of blind-man's-buff. Who wears the blindfold?

Creech must settle or be damned. Composed and delivered a searing remonstrance. Business that could have been dispatched in hours has kept me four months without the shadow of activity other than me waiting at the door. This bodes ill for my removing one hundred miles, but I do not intend to make the experiment. He has declared himself my patron and my friend – in that order – so let him vindicate this public claim, not trifle with a poor man in what touches the very quick of his existence. I laid down sentences in heat and sealed before I could be brought to reconsider.

Returning with the day still young, I pulled my chair towards the fire and composed the sweetest, fullest encomium of love. My invention soared beyond sour circumstance, last night's uneasy passages, the harsh decree of fate and so on and so forth, to consecrate the airy imagination of the goddess who brings such beings together in the higher harmony. For a moment I felt transcendent, rising above yesterday's hesitations and constraints. Taking Clarinda by the hand, we wandered on an elevated path, both in draft and fair copy.

I was invited out to dinner with Johnson and Maestro Schetskl. My inspiration continued and he promised to set 'Clarinda, Mistress of my Soul' to music. Consequently I was compelled to put the finishing touches to my 'Epistle of Love' late after plying a hearty bowl since dinner. Yet I flatter myself the style is unaffected. No distinct idea of anything at the last other than that I drank her health repeatedly. You are all my soul holds dear in this frail world.

Interleaved letter from Sylvander to Clarinda headed 'Unlavish Wisdom'.

I have been tasking my reason, Clarinda, why a woman, who, for native genius, poignant wit, strength of mind, generous sincerity of soul, and the sweetest female tenderness is without a peer; and whose personal charms have few, very few parallels among her sex; why, or how, she should fall to the blessed lot of a poor harum-scarum poet, whom Fortune has kept for her particular use to wreak her temper on whenever she is in ill-humour.

Once I conjectured that, as Fortune is the most capricious jade ever known, she may have taken a fit of remorse, nay a paroxysm of whim, to raise the poor devil out of the mire where he had so often, and so conveniently, served her as a stepping-stone. And then to give him the most glorious boon she ever had in gift, merely for the maggot's sake, to see how his fool head and his fool heart bear it.

At other times I was vain enough to think that Nature, who has a great deal to do with Fortune, had

*given the coquettish goddess some such hint as – 'Here
is a paragon of female excellence, whose equal I never
was lucky enough to hit on in my earlier compositions,
and despair of ever doing so again. You have cast her
rather in the shades of life, but there is a certain poet
of my making, and among your frolics, it would not be
amiss to attach him to this masterpiece, to give her that
immortality among mankind, which no woman of any
age ever more deserved, and which few rhymesters of
this age are better able to confer.'*

*I have written out my last sheet of paper, so I am
reduced to a half sheet. I have often amused myself with
visionary schemes of what happiness might be enjoyed
by small alterations, not in another world of which
we have hardly any idea, but in this present state of
existence.*

*For instance, imagine you and I just as we are at
present – the same reasoning powers, sentiments and
curiosity. Then imagine our bodies free from pain,
the wants of nature readily to hand. Next, we are set
free from the laws of gravitation, able to fly with ease
through all the unconjectured bounds, the recesses
of creation. What a life of bliss we would lead in our
pursuit of virtue and knowledge, our mutual enjoyment
of friendship and love.*

*I see you laughing at my fairy fancies, and calling
me a voluptuous Mahometan, but I should be a happy
creature, and it would be a congenial paradise to you
too. Can't you see us hand in hand, or my arm about
your lovely waist, making our observations on Sirius,
or surveying a flaming comet, or in a shady bower of
Venus dedicating the hour to love, while the most exalted
strains of poesy and harmony would be the spontaneous*

language of our souls.

*Devotion is the favourite employment of your heart;
so it is of mine. What greater power and incentive to
praise, in all the fervour of adoration, that Being, whose
unsearchable wisdom and goodness has pervaded every
sense, every feeling, every instinct of our higher selves.*

*You will be blessing the neglect of the maid who left
me destitute of paper.*

SYLVANDER

Out of the depths, to thee I cry.

Unable to face food or drink. Anchored to the shitting
stool, and passing blood amidst the freely flowing faeces.

Why are good fellowship and noble amity pursued by
dire disturbers and destroyers? God bless Betty and her
cordials, a present help in trouble.

Back to bed raw and scadded, till noon brought an
emissary from the goddess. Clarinda's Jenny.

Why had I not noticed Jenny properly before? More
than in the passing I mean. She had seemed a plain bush
in the shade of Clarinda's bloom. But standing there in
the window light I saw slim elegance, graceful poise, neat
fair features, red-gold hair and two steady light blue eyes.
In that gaze I shed days of morose reflection, and all the
discomforts of this morning after. With one blink, I was
back in Mauchline.

'Well, Jenny, what's your business?'

'Ah hae a letter, sir.'

'From your mistress?'

'Aye.'

'Thank you kindly.'

I threw the packet onto my table.

'Have you always lived in Edinburgh?'

'Na, ah'm frae Leith an ah'm ganging that gait noo an mistress askit me fur tae tak yer letter.'

'Excellent. And will you be coming back from Leith today?'

'Aye.'

'So you can call in for my reply.'

'If that's whit ye want.'

'It is, Jenny, truly what I want.'

'Verra weill.'

'Right then.'

And with that she was off like a young gazelle unable to stand a moment longer, hair glinting in the sun. What a waking call for any young huntsman of the name.

There were three notes in Clarinda's bundle written one upon the other. Like a player dealing cards, I read them in turn. Damn and blast her for an ungrateful hussy. How dare she turn canting moralist now, clumping over exalted ground with iron-soled boots. God forgive me, but at times she's like the milk-eyed cow that one moment gazes in liquid devotion, and the next lifts her tail in the air to skitter in all directions.

Yet how these gentrified sneerers dress up their tortured self-denial in the garments of philosophy – she has 'received a summons from Conscience to appear at the bar of Reason'.

The long and short of it is, she is neither well nor happy. Her heart reproaches her – aye, and me too – for Wednesday. I must now determine against everything except what strictest delicacy warrants, or she will not see me on Saturday. What does that make me – a peasant churl, a clumsy oaf in my Lady's boudoir? She'd be nane the waur o a guid fuck.

Of course she tries to soften it by blaming herself but the implication is clear, she gives the game away with every sanctimonious line. By Thursday night, she urges friendship with God as our chief study and delight. This damnable aetherial notion of religion satisfies neither heart nor the belly. Sacred ties that unite – unite what? Two wraiths in the sky?

Clarinda dearest, do you think I could forget – has she ever let me forget – that her present and eternal happiness depend upon her adherence to virtue. Happiness at least when measured by worldly and not heavenly approval. Is that sufficient reason to put me on the rack? 'Happy Sylvander' – my God, happy – that can be attached to Heaven and to Clarinda together. She at least cannot serve two masters.

At the hinnerend she prays over me – last thing last night or first this morning – petitioning a place for the poet in God's bosom, and next a place for the tender charities of parent, brother, child. By Christ, I need no lesson in these charities. As for bosom, I would rather put my hands full on hers, and end this melancholy hysteria with frank acknowledged desire. Finally, she sends the whole extended tract round with Jenny – 'who is a good soul'. Just in case I expected an infernal messenger.

By mid afternoon my ravings receded and I crafted some pleas in reply. How could she wound my soul in such a fashion and wish the hour of parting sooner? If I have trespassed against decorum's letter, where have I sinned against the spirit of her statutes?

My whole appeal, Clarinda, to God, yourself and to me, be reconciled. Do not divide us by distrust, or raise false barriers against the innermost sensibilities. They are the divine essence of love and friendship. Do not destroy our peace by torturing your or my love.

Unable to cap such a flourish, I proposed a visit tomorrow with Ainslie, who is desperate to see her though he can only stay a short time due to another previous engagement... She cannot resist the desire to meet 'my bosom Bob'.

Jenny returned as promised to collect my missive of mercy. We dallied a while till I proved the frankness of her look and the strength of honest desire. O, the bonny banks of Ayr flower fairer fresher than Edina's unforgiving ramparts.

Before leaving, Jenny let me know she lodged on the Cowgate near the foot of Niddrie Wynd. I knew I had seen her the other night; did she take a sighting of the poet?

Remembered at the last that this was my name day, January twenty-fifth. I was exhausted by its dispensations, as if receiving triple measure for one light passage between two darks. But all has ended in blessed relief. Let tomorrow bring what it will.

Back on an even keel this morning. Jenny was sent with a card to postpone my visit, but I dashed off a note in reply pleading Bob's disappointment. Returned the messenger with a kiss for reward.

As I expected, Nancy was charmed by Bob. There is something priestly in the way he bends a sympathetic ear, dips and nods his approbation. She thawed, then warmed with a confiding manner, seasoned by some gentle teasing. He was instantly smitten; I could see the signs. Had I not reminded him an hour later about his urgent appointment, he would have been drooling still.

As for me, I rested content in this renewed cordiality.

We chatted like old admirers and I took my leave with a friendly kiss. All was natural and unforced at the end.

Took myself off to Niddrie Wynd, where I was amused to find that Jenny Clow resides in the same close as Jessie Haws. She has her own little chamber there in the attics where we could be private and unrestrained. Bit by bit, with lavish persuasions, I uncovered the body of a Venus beneath the plain cloth. I believe that Jenny is no stranger to the other sex, but for the first time I acquainted her with real female pleasure.

Up with the lark to make my morning obeisance. Wrote to Clarinda in the same spirit of devotion. Last night we kindled a new happiness, but at a flame of innocence where Honour stands by as a sacred guard. Onto that sanctuary I cannot trespass: no one who loves as I love would make such an angel miserable.

Went on to wait on Miss Nimmo's friend Mrs Stewart, whose husband may carry some influence with the Excise. In her cold drawing room I was questioned like a child about my life, and roundly chided for scratching some Jacobite lines on an inn window. O naughty poet – the sheer presumption. How is it the great of this world feel called not only to deafen us with the din of their entourage, but to lecture us on their superior wisdom? I could have laughed in her porridgy face but kept strict control of my tongue.

Then I called round on Miss Nimmo, dear soul, to thank her for her good offices. How was she to know that Mrs S is a right royal fart. She prattled on kindly and restored my good humour.

Schektl has done his music for the Clarinda setting

and it is apt and enlivening. I must encourage Johnson to draw in more composers rather than depend solely on traditional airs. Kept sounding it through for the rest of the day, humming with my usual lumpen pitch.

Prayed again this Sabbath evening for Nancy. My sincere self-denial as regards Clarinda has released a spring of spiritual enthusiasm deep in my soul.

Thou Almighty Author of peace and goodness, and love, do thou give me the social heart that kindly tastes of every man's cup? Is it a draught of joy? Warm and open my heart to share it with cordial unenvious rejoicing. Is it the bitter potion of sorrow? Melt my heart with sympathetic woe.

Above all, do thou give me the manly mind, that resolutely exemplifies in life and manners those sentiments which I would wish to be thought to possess. The friend of my soul – there may I never deviate from firmest fidelity and most active kindness. Clarinda, dear object of my fondest love – there may the most sacred inviolate honour, the most faithful kindling constancy, ever watch over and animate my every thought and imagination.

Snow last night, frozen hard this morning. So I extracted Bob and Willie from their duties. We walked out to Duddingston, icy snow crunching underfoot and the old hill capped in white. To the south I could see the rigs furrowed with the lie of the land but smoothed out by this winter covering. I could feel the adamantine earth below my hands, chilled by thoughts of unremitting labour. How could I go back to such a life, wresting a poor recompense from unyielding nature. But when we followed the track round the shoulder of the hill, a joyful scene met our eyes. The loch was frozen over, bizzing with skaters and burnished bright by curlers' brooms. Braziers cheered the icy banks and sliding stones were urged on not just by sweeping brushes, but by wild cries stoked with regular applications of warming flasks. What a tumbling, shouting, playing press of cloud-breathing humanity.

We stood and watched till we began to lose sensation in our feet. So we repaired to the Sheep's Heid for mutton stew laced with brandies. How I wished poor Fergusson, my brother in the Muse, could be one of our party – to hear how he would catch this day of roister-rouster in tangy feisty verse. A Hyperborean Bacchanal.

> Auld Reikie, thourt the canty hole
> A bield for mony caldrife soul,
> Wha snugly at thine ingle loll,
> Baith warm and couth;
> While round they gar the bicker roll
> To weet their mouth.

We slipped and stumbled hame. I mark this day down for the calendar of precious times that should ever be remembered, never cast into the grey oblivion of lost moments, forgotten selves.

Another from Clarinda awaited my return. Long and in two parts. She is pleased to be my friend but when I come across her mind as a lover she has a sting of guilt. Scanning this early sentence, I put the thing aside. Would anyone not weary of this one-note melody?

Considered a visit to the Cowgate but was too cold and wet to venture out again. So took a final warming glass, and composed myself to consider Brodie's offer which I have neglected. Not to mention Creech.

Sober reflections. Day comes more iron-grey than light.

Are we ever free in life to make choices worthy of our deeper truer selves?

Clarinda bound in iron bands. Another man's wife. Why should her destiny, or that of any woman, be determined by the whim of a creature such as McLehose? Yet she is hemmed in on all sides.

On Sunday, it seems she consulted with Reverend Kemp and confessed to receiving a tender impression. It seemed natural that she should unbosom herself, and no doubt he was very obliging. Like a benevolent parent, Kemp urged only friendship, given her situation. 'Should I mention this to my special friend?' she went on to ask. Unbosom, then, to Cousin William! 'Not at all,' counsels the wily Kemp, 'since you are not bound to him by any formal tie.' Only the tie of craven dependence!

Poor Nancy. A woman made to give and to receive love is confined in her museum case of dusty respectability. Cousin William is to call on her today. Has he sniffed some gossip?

Meanwhile Clarinda wants me to meet with Mr Kemp. Heaven help us, she sees in him my perfect other half. The bird can sing in her cage but only blindfolded.

As for Brodie in his den, he exercises power by preying on man's greed and cruelty. Yet I wonder what turned someone raised in privilege and moral superiority so completely to the night. Is he in some obscure fashion a victim too? Is his the necessary shadow to Edinburgh's daylight?

I should spurn this connection outright but... to trace the Deacon's life, as I did for Clarinda and she for me... would that untangle the roots of good and ill, or bury them beyond discovery? Could a poetic form tell the tale while keeping the hero's identity a secret – or should I turn novelist? Imagine the reaction were the Deacon to appear, masked, before the Edinburgh public in a stage play. He who must not be named.

Tomorrow I will summon some energy and call on Mr Brodie, before attending the court of Clarinda. She wants me to take my chance at half past eight, for she is expiring from want of knowing what Ainslie thinks of her. I shall dangle a smitten Bob before her claws.

Waited on Creech once more at his place of business in the Luckenbooths. Business, though, may be a miscalling since nothing appears further from his mind or conversation. It was as if our exchange of letters had never been. Instead he took it on himself to announce me in the shop and praise my Elegy on Lord President Dundas. This for him exemplifies poetry's highest strain – propping up the great and powerful.

Next Creech will propose a second Edinburgh Edition of Robert Burns with the elegy and any other meagre works I have produced, all subscribed within his existing copyright. For which I am still unpaid! Curse Creech and all his kind. I will never pen another poem here except a last farewell.

As for the Dundas dynasty, they have given not a jot of notice to my verses. Poetry attracts their disdain but for the poet they have only contempt; I am beneath notice. Every time now that I see the name Dundas in the column of a newspaper, my heart constricts. I feel my forehead flush and my lip quiver.

Yet I will not be put down by their ilk. My songs will lend the people's voice a hearing. Those who dine on homely fare and wear the hodden grey will not bend the knee forever to burkies who strut to display their worthless baubles. A man's a man for all that. And Creech will pay his full dues to the poet whatever it takes.

Fortified my stirring resolutions with Johnson at Dowie's, and then proceeded to the Deacon's caverns in the late afternoon. When I asked to see him, glances were exchanged and going down the passage I brushed against two burly fellows hurrying up the way. They looked the other way.

Himself seemed slightly disconcerted, but I took the initiative and asked about his life and upbringing. Gradually he relaxed and answered my questions plainly without touching on the central mystery. He seems free of remorse and proud of the secret influence he wields. Could he exert some pressure on Creech if I asked? I gave him to understand that I was still considering his proposal and would remain entirely confidential. For his part, the Deacon repeated his mantra, 'Don't delay, Mr Burns, who knows what tomorrow holds for you or me?' The gambler's instinct for blind chance, or some dark foreknowing? For him or me?

As before, I left the Deacon in need of ready cheer, so I looked in at Niddrie's Wynd to see if Jenny had lowsed from work. I found her and Jessie very chief together in the Haw's ground floor room. They both seemed pleased to see me, and Jessie gave me a wink to let me know she knew, while on the other side Jenny winked to let me know that Jessie knew. No doubt they had spent an hour already winking to each other. Nothing would do but that I take them both to Clartie's, one on either side, for stovies with hot toddies. Thus genial Nature provides the remedy for January's chills. Nonetheless, I felt an icy dart when I began to take my leave. Handsome Jenny looked me boldly in the eye as if to say she knew where I was calling; and why should I prefer the yea and nay of Mistress Nancy's manners to her frank embrace. I had no reply to give, so I paid and went back into the Cowgate.

I found Clarinda tearful and disposed to collapse. This was a different face, so I cradled her in my arms and let her sobs exhaust themselves against my consoling warmth. I remembered holding some distressed lamb in this way at my mother's fireside.

Gradually she calmed, so I offered more substantial comfort, easing her bosom and caressing her hips and thighs with gentle motions. She clung closer, turning her body into mine till I found her mouth moist and open to my lips. She pressed down on my knees and I moved my hand to the seat of her desire. For one sweet moment we were joined in precious union. But I dared go no further for fear of destroying such blissful release. We sat for a long time leaning on each other as the glow receded. Neither of us spoke.

Finally I raised her to her feet and kissed her farewell. Her cheeks were bathed in tears but I fancied they were not all of sadness. As I turned to go my own eyes were filled to overflowing.

Now, Clarinda, I should lay down my pen and close this journal, since I believe sincerely that Heaven has nothing more to give us on this earth. Ae fond kiss and then we parted. The rest should be silence.

Prince Charles Edward Stewart died yesterday in exile. Nicol came round to give me the news and we went out to a gathering in the Prince's honour. Songs and toasts. Scotland would be the poorer in music were it not for the

Bonnie Pretender. Yet his passing also ends the hope of Restoration. Are Scotland's ancient freedoms finally lost, buried and lamented?

> Here Stewarts once in triumph reigned
> And laws for Scotland's weal ordained.
> But now unroofed their palace stands,
> Their sceptre fall'n to other hands;
> Fallen indeed and to the earth
> Whence grovelling reptiles take their birth.
> The injured Stewart line are gone,
> A race outlandish fill their throne;
> An idiot race to honour lost
> Who know them best despise them most.

True when I scratched it on Stirling's window and still true now, whatever the unbearable Mrs Whoever and the whole Excise Board direct against me. The Jacobite cause is the good old cause of Scotland herself, and my family at least have stood by it with unflinching loyalty. According to Clarinda she would have schooled me against the inscription, but anyway perhaps I would be better off without an Excise Commission – more free from temptation. So one aside reveals the woman's breeding from the top of her curly head to the tip of her dainty toe.

Went on from our melancholy carousal to Jenny early in the evening. I explained the delicate issue of my friendship with her mistress to her entire satisfaction, on one principal count at least.

Then I proved my undying love for her in the most exemplary fashion.

Came home to a further eloquent missive from Clarinda. Resolved to copy out one glowing passage, for neither

Thomson nor Shenstone have exceeded her on the theme of Platonic love. Other matter here for another day. She goes to Miers tomorrow for her silhouette. Unchaperoned, she is unquestioned. I will wear her on a breast-pin next my heart.

Busy at correspondence most of today. Rain and sleet had washed away all the season's brightness.

Wrote to my Lord Glencairn asking him to secure me the Excise Commission. I cannot delay this any longer as everything at home is out of sorts. Glencairn is my lodestone, my morning star. Without his generous support my poetry would be unknown beyond Ayrshire. But he will not approve the Excise scheme for his ploughman poet.

God knows, I barely approve myself, yet how else can I save the little home that shelters an aged mother, two brothers and three sisters from destruction. Gilbert's lease is wretched but after what I have given and will give, he will weather the remaining seven years.

That will leave me two, maybe three hundred pounds. If Creech pays to the full I should have at least five hundred. Instead of beggaring myself with another small farm, I could deposit my little stock in a banking house and keep the ghost of wasting sorrow from my door. And Jean's, God help her.

For once, I can grasp the anchor of sober mature deliberation; and I shall leave no stone unturned to put it into practice. But I must have that Commission! So I turn with sincerity to Glencairn, who rescued me first from obscurity, wretchedness and exile.

I enclosed a copy of 'Holy Willie' which he will enjoy, knowing that these verses will never be exposed to public view, and that if they were the noble earl would be constrained to disown them and their author outright. His Lordship kens what it is to have the Presbyterian curs yapping at your heels.

Should have written yesterday to Clarinda, so I dated my reply for last night. She has asked my advice about Cousin William. A kittle matter, since on her own admission she has given her various friends different confidences.

Instant gelding is my judgement on this pawing benefactor.

Nancy is a woman framed for friendship with the lesser sex – no woman ever so entirely stormed my soul. But now it appears that for at least a year Craig, her intimate protector, has had his own designs. Subtle insinuations, looks, accidental touches, which she has fended off without compromising her dependence on his generosity. I smelled out the way his wind was blowing from the first.

She cannot feel for Cousin Craig as he deserves (I could give him his just desserts) but does he understand that? She thinks not. Meanwhile the unctuous Kemp has received (mouth agape or I'll be damned) Nancy's declaration of fond feeling for an unnamed friend.

Has she given Kemp to believe it may be Craig? Hence the further difficulty of confiding in Craig about the unnamed one, in case he tells Kemp who then realises Craig is not in fact the man. This would then unleash the bloodhounds of the drawing room.

She knows she must not unleash the green-eyed monster to plague her placid cousin; yet Clarinda asks my agreement to this very course of action. My advice is of no consequence. Her request is a tactful way of apprising me of her full situation, which after all is not of my making. She wants my absolute discretion and will have it to full measure. Why would I care to expose or embarrass her?

I could reply outlining by subtle indirection the complications that ensure my complete silence, though I am unwilling to play that hand since it would end this game forever, and I am fondly attached. Rather, I affirm her right and need to bestow allegiance wherever her heart inclines. And if cruel circumstance debars her from open avowal, then let affection flourish in the privacy of her soul and parlour. Nancy owes nothing to the society that has given her or her sex so little except painful humiliation. That is a theme Tom Paine and the liberty pamphlets should consider.

What at the last is her obligation to McLehose? No doubt in Jamaica he indulges every freedom of his sex. And here in Edinburgh her mother's cousin, Lord Dreghorn the Judge, disdains to acknowledge her, as if she were outcast, deranged, or worse. These are the true haters of women, who seize their illicit pleasure and then persecute their victims like a contagion of evil. May woman curse and blast them. May her lovely hand shut rapture's portal inexorably in their face. May their declining years deliver palsy, gout and wasted powers to every vital organ. Then let her cast open the beautiful gate to tantalise and ravish their impotent desires. Gelding is too merciful and too quick.

Clarinda needs above all else her friend and protector, a companion and lover. Why cannot I be that man, even if Bob must sometimes stand in the place of friend?

Having dispatched last night's letter, I turned unsociable. So wrote up this day's journal before supper and my departure for Potterrow.

Some evenings are snatched from time into a higher sphere. Such was last night's visit. We were harmonious and unconstrained as all true friends should be, yet today I feel that something precious is slipping from me. Were these by some cruel design our final hours? I have copied out Clarinda's words of comfort in the hope that they will turn back the mortal tide.

Sylvander, I believe our friendship will be lasting; its basis has been virtue, similarity of tastes, feelings, and sentiments. Alas, I shudder at the idea of one hundred miles' distance. You'll hardly write me once a month, and other objects will weaken your affection for Clarinda. Yet I cannot believe so. Let the scenes of Nature remind you of Clarinda! In winter, remember the dark shades of her fate; in summer, the cordial warmth of her friendship; in autumn her glowing wishes to bestow plenty on all kinds or conditions; and let spring animate you with hopes that your friend may yet live to surmount the wintry blasts of life, and revive to taste a springtime of happiness.

At all events, the storms of life will quickly pass, and 'one unbounded Spring encircle all'. There, Sylvander, I trust we will meet. Love there is not a crime. I charge you to meet me there – O God, I must lay down my pen—

She must not lay down her pen – look, I take it in my own hand – for she has the key to my heart as I have of hers. May my hand wither, if I deviate from the firmest fidelity and most active kindness, whatever the future holds.

Yet today I confess that I have looked through 'the dark postern of time long elapsed'. And it was a rueful prospect. What a tissue of thoughtlessness, weakness and folly. My days are like a ruined temple. Strength and proportion can still be discerned in some segments, but torn gaps and prostrate ambition prevail. I kneel before the Parent of all mercies. 'Father, I have sinned against Heaven and in Thy sight, and am no more worthy to be called thy son.'

I rose eased and strengthened; while I despise the superstition of the fanatic, I love the religion of humanity. The years stretch out before me and I must 'on reason build resolve, that column of true majesty in man'.

Once again I felt disinclined to company, but Nicol drove me out. And now the scales have truly fallen from my sadly disillusioned eyes. All the coarse pleasures of the town assailed me like a filthy violent mob – the raucous merriment, drunkards' piss running in the street, painted whores and the Deacon's minions lurking in the shadow to leap out and drag me down. Only the godly stand apart, fortified by locks, barred doors and shutters.

What luxury of bliss I was enjoying at this time last night. Clarinda has stolen away my soul but she has refined, exalted it. From her I have received a stronger sense of virtue and a manlier spirit of piety. When a poet and a poetess of Nature's making drink together from the cup of love and bliss, let not the coarse stuff of humankind profanely measure what they can never know. Clarinda, first of your sex, if ever I forget you, if ever your lovely image is effaced from my inner eye, 'May I be lost, no eye to weep my end; and find no earth that's base enough to bury me.'

Early up and dressed like any respectable citizen on his way to church. The odours and offal of last night seemed forgotten, washed away by a showery blast. As I came into the Tron Kirk the first psalm was put up.

Come let us to the Lord our God
With contrite hearts return
Our God is gracious nor will leave
The desolate to mourn.

What can match the dignity and emotion of an auld Scots psalm? The prayers began; scripture reading beckoned. My eye began to wander across the boxed pews, everyone ordered in their proper place and degree. As the prayer concluded, I saw Clarinda's fair head rise. A severely tied bonnet could not repress wholly the tumble of her curls. Her liquid eyes gazed down demurely. But mine went up to the pulpit where Kemp presided, a striking figure, tall, with flowing locks and a sweeping command. He is the perfect guide and spiritual guardian of his flock.

'Let me live the life of the righteous, and my latter end be like His.' This was his text. Who are the righteous? Those whose minds are governed by purity, truth and charity. But where does such a mind exist? It can only be where the soul is perfect. But Kemp knows none such on earth. The righteous then must mean those who believe in Christ and rely on His perfect righteousness for their salvation. And so forth, in the well oiled groove.

The sermoniser embarked on the full flow of logic-chopping eloquence, defining, categorising, excluding, all with expansive or decisive gestures and a roving eye to calculate the effect. The actor is hard pressed to match such conscious art. Some gazed up hanging on every clause; others stared stolidly at the pew in front.

I remained discreetly at the rear, preparing to withdraw unobserved, but as I rose to leave, my eye lit on a familiar face at the front of a side aisle. He sat rigidly upright and looked ahead proudly, every bit the Deacon of Trades. My movement seemed to catch his eye. The basilisk turned in my direction with an unblinking stare. Had he recognised me? The psalm was called and people stood blocking his view. I slipped away.

Outside, the showers had blown away to Fife. I fetched Jenny to walk out to the sea shore. Though her father had come to Leith for work, my Jenny was born at Fisherrow, so she knows all the paths and byways past Craigmillar Castle and down to the sea. The wind whipped up white horses as we stepped out along the shoreline. My leg behaved as if fully restored.

She chattered on about the fisher-folk. Her mother's people are still fishwives carrying a day's catch in great creels on their back up to Edinburgh. What price for men's lives? The fishers are a close-knit clan, marrying always inside the group – Fisherrow foreign to Newhaven and Newhaven to Granton. Jenny misses that in Edinburgh, where everyone looks out only for themselves. How true.

There is something frank and natural about Jenny Clow with her glinting hair tied tightly back, and her glowing skin chafed to life by sea and sun.

We went on to Musselburgh and stopped at an inn. My leg was stiffening so I hired a gig back to town, and Jenny laughed the whole way at the rattling clattering motion, and the view flying by through the rain. I went in at Niddrie Wynd to make a happy end to our day, bundled together like lovers in the country way.

Whatever happened to Rab of Mossgiel and his innocent wooings? How much longer must I thole this place?

Feverish night, and awoke all aches from my soaking. Strange dream in which I was standing in Professor

Fergusson's drawing room. A young boy was pointing at a picture depicting a soldier's lass weeping oer the body of her fallen love in the snow. 'Oh but he was bonny,' she cried, 'the bonniest man that e'er I saw with his broad brow and dark flashing eyes, he was the one for me, my own ploughman lad.' This is the recollection of some true incident but in my dream the lass was Jenny and I was bleeding to death on the wintry ground.

Laid low for the day with *Amelia*, but went to Clarinda's as arranged. The youngsters were just settled so we had to converse in whispers. The mood was querulous and off-key. When I complained of our hardships, she took it personally. Tears and headaches.

Why are women called the tender sex when I have never met one who can repay me in passion? They are either defaulters like Creech, or niggards where I bestow freely. Retreated to St James Square for hot toddie and the promise of renewing sleep.

Sent round my apologies first thing with a promise to come round later and make up. About nine o'clock, which gives me time to call in on Jenny.

Dispatched notes to Nasmith, Schektl, Miers and others pleading my last week and sociable necessity.

Nothing from the Excise. Nothing from Creech. So called in at the shop to announce my departure. The old fox looked astonished, as if life beyond Edinburgh were a mirage, and shuffled papers in order to signal urgent attention to my business. I bore the whole performance with resignation.

Clarinda was calm and a little flirtatious, as if this were our first and not our final week. Gave her Peggy's letters to read as a peace offering. In reply she dangles a smitten Mary Peacock before me, as I dangle Bob. Now the circle of gossip is four rather than two, not counting Jenny. How long can a secret be known and still kept? Anyway, Mary Peacock is as appetising as watery gruel.

Off to an artists' dinner at the Baronet's. God bless Nasmith and the rest for honest esteem and good fellowship. Ayrshire is bereft of such convivial companionship.

Slight head but nothing incapacitating.

If I cannot have the Commission, I must have the farm. Wrote John Tennant to go with me and inspect Ellisland. He will do it for my father's sake as well as mine.

Also wrote Richmond in Mauchline to see if I could get any more news of Jean. Gilbert is silent as a sphinx, a sure sign he has got the money.

Clarinda finds Miss Chalmers' letters charming. *Why did not such a woman secure your hand? It is the caprice of human nature, particularly the female variety, to fix upon impossibilities.* Quite. Mrs McLehose will keep for tomorrow.

Headed into town to rustle up Willie and Nicol. The former is sunk deep in his encyclopaedias, while the latter is moroser than Ovid in the Black Sea. Forced them both to Dowie's to engage in conversation. Do they not realise that their boon companion is close to banishment? Will Smellie come afarming or Nicol engage in a Dumfriesshire tour? I doubt them both, whatever glass they raise in pledge. As for Bob, mewling or purring, he would not survive a staging-post beyond Auld Reikie. As it transpired, he came in later, wearing his heart on his sleeve while trying assiduously to conceal it beneath his coat.

Jenny was closed to visitors. Belly-aching, confided Jessie Haws as doorkeeper. Chatted awhile then scouted the Cowgate, eyes averted from Hastie's Close. I have no wish to talk theology with Mr Brodie. Home again intact, though limping once more due to last Sunday's exertions.

Dreich and inclement weather. Schektl's melody has been running through my mind like a babbling burn all week, but my third verse was clumsy. Prepared an improved version for presentation to Clarinda in the evening.

Clarinda, mistress of my soul,
The measured time is run!
The wretch beneath the dreary pole,
So marks the latest sun.

To what dark care of frozen night
Shall poor Sylvander hie;
Deprived of thee, his life and light,
The Sun of all his joy.

We part – but by these precious drops,
That fill thy lovely eyes,
No other light shall guide my steps,
Till thy bright beams arise.

She, the fair Sun of all her sex,
Has blest my glorious day:
And shall a glimmering Planet fix
My worship to its ray.

Hopefully there is still time to correct Johnson's proofs. The lady herself was more subdued yet quietly affectionate. The storms and even the squalls have abated leaving us drifting in divergent streams, becalmed and exhausted. Home to prayers and to rest.

Called for Jenny just after noon when I knew she would be finished at Potterrow. As the day was better, we walked out. I did not want to go far so we turned up the High Street towards the Castle. Why should the poet be shamed to promenade through the Lawnmarket with a serving-lass on his arm?

Castlehill was busy with families and courting couples taking the caller air. The trees are bare so the prospect out to hills and the salt-crested firth was clear and bright.

Jenny asked me about home and my family. I told her about our farms and my father's early death. She listened quietly and intently. I told her too about Jean, though not about our summer or the present hardships.

'Whit wey did she no want tae mairry oan you?' Jenny asked, sounding like her mistress about Jean and Peggy Chalmers.

'Her father wouldn't hae it.'

'He wouldna hae stappit me,' she rejoined firmly, 'I'd hae rin awa frae the auld bugger.'

I laughed and pressed her to my side. We wandered back down to the Grassmarket and took some refreshment at the White Hart. I nodded to a few acquaintances but stayed close to Jenny. This was our day.

We went along the Cowgate to Niddrie's Wynd as the day began to fail. She lit a fire in the little attic room and sat on my knee. Then she took off her shawl and dress to let me trace the shapes of her warming body. The skin was smooth and shiny without blemish. She said I was her ain bonny man.

We lay down together and made love slowly, gently. Afterwards I stayed by her side and told her that I would be leaving this week. But that I would come back soon.

She cried with hard, fierce sobs. When I tried to comfort, she turned her back to me, face to the wall, and refused speech. I got up and left saying that I would come to see her during the week. Why is it that I feel more sorrow for myself than pity for her distress?

Immobile all day. Saw no one. Let them go to Kirk or Hell. What do I care?

Johnson rescued me early. He needs a preface now for the second volume – excited and suddenly urgent, he almost dragged me out of bed. Sat down at the table and penned a glowing commendation. Here, volume by volume, are all the Scots songs – those already with music and others now set to melodies. The treasures of a people and of a nation. These books will outlive us all, and Johnson will be remembered with gratitude.

Still low but today the corpse stirred.

Down sharp to the printer's shop to correct the sheets as they came off. I have my own stool there since the Edinburgh book, and a grudging respect from the setters, engravers and binders. They know my corrections to be swift and sure. Feeding back the sheets, I worked without a rest till the job was done. Honest toil amidst honest men. Johnson flapped around like a mother hen crazed by anxiety for her hatching chicks. Eventually I oxtered him off to Dowie's to calm him down and let the job go forward.

No heart for social visits. Came back to count my remaining coins, and write a long diligent reply to a letter from Mrs Dunlop. Hoping to call at Dunlop House on my way home, so I reported the social tittle-tattle to my dear guide in matters of etiquette and morals, and enclosed 'Clarinda, Mistress of My Soul'. She may become my Ayrshire Clarinda, one without the curls, the lashes or the swelling bosom.

The great book is ready – crisp and fresh on every newly cut page, all sheets upstanding between their handsome covers. Willie McElheney, a Belfast man lost in Edinburgh, pulled out a bottle of Bushmills whisky to handsel the new arrivals.

Returned home to think who should be sent a copy. This at least has not been loss or waste. Creech must not know how deep I am in this venture; Johnson will have the credit. No message from Clarinda.

The *Museum's* dinner becomes my farewell to Edinburgh. I must name the day.

Later. Clarinda letter arrived as I left for dinner. The cat is out of our bag; the squalling commences with a vengeance.

She wants to break it off, never to see me again. The reason? A letter from Kemp expressing his and Craig's concerns for her reputation and virtue. They are the elders to her Susannah. Arse-faced bastards, farting from every orifice. They crash into a secluded garden shaded with delicacy, truth and honour and dump a load of ill-smelling shite in the midst. Let the bigots stuff it down their own throats till they choke and spew.

God help Clarinda. The tone is haughty and dictatorial. She must end forever such an unsuitable relationship. With whom though? It seems that they know not the man. Or surely they would have named me – the summit of obloquy in this tight-arsed town.

Who gives a fellow creature, one who is neither her peer nor capable of being her judge, the right to catechise, scold, demean, abuse and insult, wantonly insult? Is it because she is a woman who cannot take a blade and thrust it into their stinking entrails?

To hell with them. I must put my case to Clarinda. Have we been called to a sacred court or to the bar of reason that entitles dissolution of our union? No, their appeal is to base convention, not the higher truths that we have tasted together. Surely she sees that she is not under the slightest shadow of obligation to bestow her love, tenderness, caresses, affections, heart and soul on one who has habitually and barbarously broken every tie of nature, duty and gratitude to his faithful spouse? How then can it be improper to give that heart and those affections to another, when by so doing she harms neither children, herself or society at large?

I was still composing these pleas when another letter arrived from Potterrow. I opened this new packet with trepidation. Now her distress pours out. How will she manage with the loss of friendship and support from her two principal guardians? How can I comfort her when I am the cause of her injury? Nancy, Nancy, how can I wish I had never seen you, that we had never met? Not while I live and breathe. Yet now it appears I am leaving her friendless.

I sat down to write again moderating my spleen, softening my argument less it affront her alarmed sensibility. I plead forgiveness for the injury and promise to be with her tonight. No sooner had this gone than another arrived from Clarinda written earlier than her last. Such are the vagaries of the penny post. I felt calmer now, pulling back from the brink and able to state our situation with greater clarity and dignity, as befits two natures such as ours.

I met you, my dear Clarinda, by far the first of womankind, at least to me. I esteemed, I loved you at first sight, both of which attachments you have done me the honour to return. The longer I am acquainted with you, the more innate worth I discover in you.

You have suffered a loss, I confess, for my sake; but if the firmest, steadiest, warmest friendship; if every endeavour to be worthy of your friendship; if a love, strong as the ties of nature, and holy as the duties of religion; if all these can make anything like a compensation for the evil I have occasioned you; if they be worth your acceptance, or can in the least add to your enjoyments – so help Sylvander, you Powers above, in his hour of need, as he freely gives all these to Clarinda!

I esteem you, I love you, as a friend; I admire you, I love you, as a woman, beyond any in the circle of creation. I know I shall continue to admire you, to love you, to pray for you, nay, to pray for myself for your sake.

Dispatched and ate a hurried lunch at home, awaiting any further revelations. I take up the *Museum* and turn its pages with a soothing satisfaction. Here is contained the anonymous genius of a nation, but also songs by Smollett, Ramsay, Hamilton of Gilbertfield, Fergusson, Ossian MacPherson, Dr Blacklock, and Robert Burns. Here too is 'Cauld Kail in Aberdeen' as revised by the D— of G—, and two songs 'By a Lady'. So I immortalise Nancy's poetic gift. A fair exchange for shaking off the slimy Kemp and confidential Craig.

Write to John Skinner enclosing Volume Two with my compliments. Old Tullochgorum will weigh its true worth. Also requested five songs for Volume Three.

Another letter, but from Graham of Fintry assuring me of a Commission in the Excise. The die is cast. But at least my begging days are done.

Later. Like two brimming rivers our feelings burst their banks and flow into one united stream. That a woman lonely and forlorn, yet glowing with love and sympathy, cannot join with her soul-mate is an offence to God and Nature. We wept together and embraced. But our time was short and I slipped away in the darkness like a common criminal.

Tried to write again this morning but threw it to one side. More words are useless. Breenged out instead to face down this wretched place. What more can the stone faces inflict on me? Why should they avert their sightless gaze from me, the living man and poet? Strode up to walk on Calton Hill but sudden rage invaded me. I pulled up a sapling by the roots, and started up Leith Wynd to confront Creech and demand my payment. But I met with Ainslie and he dissuaded me. According to him, I was waving the tree and muttering 'I'll break that shite Creech's head.' He thought I had been in drink all night.

Came back and wrote in measured terms of sympathy to Nancy. The act of writing can uphold us like a ship in stormy seas.

After lunch and some small talk in the family kitchen,

I cornered Creech in his den, without the camouflage of company. Whether something desperate in my eyes or the definite date of my departure sobered him, he swore solemnly to finalise the statement and make a payment when I return in two weeks time. We went out, took tea together, and shook hands. This time I think I have him.

Looked in at Dowie's to pledge my satisfaction but my birse was up and refused to settle. Before five o'clock I was in Hastie's Close asking for the Deacon. The minions looked askance but he was clearly there in advance of some evening business and eventually I was ushered downwards.

He seemed disarranged, not his usual steely self. Was the wig awry, the hand a mite unsteady on the decanter? Perhaps I was deceived in the guttering gloom?

'Good evening to you, sir.'

'And to you, Mr Burns.'

The old formalities at least were still in place. I apologised for calling round unannounced as if we were in a Canongate mansion. Then I regretted my immediate departure from the town. This pierced his reserve.

'So, you're slinking off.'

'My business here is ended, sir.'

'And what of my business?'

'I am very sorry that I cannot make that my concern.'

The dam burst. A foul drain overflowed.

'You conceited wee puppy. Awa back to the midden whaur ye belong. Naeboby mucks aboot wi me and walks away scatheless.'

He was salivating copiously and spitting in my face with fury. I stepped back but retained my composure.

'I'm making no implication against you; I've had enough of Edinburgh.'

'Man, you're no fit tae scour the streets o Edinburgh, wi your sentimental naethins, your rights o man. It's trash, every last bit o it.'

He had a hold of my jacket now, but I believe I have his exact words.

'Believe me, Burns, the ainly thing this toun unnerstauns is power, aye an money, an if need be force tae pit fear intae their black, stinkin herts.'

With the last spitting syllable a drunken grin spread across his face, more ludicrously terrible than all his previous composure.

I shook myself free of his grip and stumbled back up the stairs. No one prevented me and within seconds I was in the Cowgate, retching against a wall. For an instant I had a mad impulse to return and tell him about my Excise Commission, but as I leant my sweating brow against the cold stone, I could hear an inner voice chanting 'a dog returning to his own vomit, own vomit, own vomit'.

I crept along the Cowgate, skulking in shadows. I had no mind for further company, yet thought if I could get to Liberton's Wynd Nicol would keep me from myself and from a bottle. Eventually to win home and write down what happened.

A defeated cur. Is that what I am, running, whining for his kennel? A dog returning to his vomit. God help me, Clarinda, and pray for me.

Shivering and sweating by turns all morning. I could feel the blood pounding in my ears, the old thorn in my chest. Betty administered broth and whisky with a liberal hand, as if she knew I would soon be out of reach.

Got myself out of bed after lunch, and forced myself to

a task. Put the Edinburgh subscribers on one side, and my list for *Scots Musical Museum* on the other. The gentlemen of the Caledonian Hunt loomed large. I persisted with a shaky hand ticking those few who merited a mint copy.

By late afternoon my quakes had subsided to quivers. Remembering the innocent pleasures of last Saturday, I ventured out to Niddre's Wynd with a cautious step. The stair was shut and deserted so I sat quietly in Dowie's till Clarinda's coast was clear. I spoke not a word to a soul and no man spoke to me. Was I already under the Deacon's prohibition?

At Potterrow I was like a familiar ghost, acknowledged but already absent. The odious Craig had been before me and consoled her on the contretemps with Kemp. She had thanked him for his visit; then he said it was to mask the change in his friendship. Mark the mealy-mouthed, smooth-tongued hypocrite. He did not name me but spoke in a way that plainly showed he knew. Such was Nancy's account. I made a semblance of deep emotion to hide my anger. We parted shortly thereafter with I believe mutual relief.

Could not abide to end the night there, so I resorted back to the Cowgate. Jessie was at her corner and I asked after my Jenny.

'She's nae weill, Maister Burns.'

'Where's she gone?'

'Awa hame, for the noo, onygates.'

I was disappointed but covered it well, joking about my broken heart. She laughed in my face and I pushed her into the close, fumbling at the jade's skirts. Another laugh as I grasped her warm buttocks but my insistence lasted only four or five quick strokes. Afterwards we lay down in her room but I could do no more tonight. She showed me out and shoved me towards St James Square.

Even Johnnie Pintle has finished with Edinburgh now. Wanted to drink brandy but it makes my pulse thump unbearably. Just glad to lie down in my own narrow bed.

Betty packed my few clothes and books. I promised to be back soon. 'Aye weill, ye'll nae be sae blate,' she chided, sponging me down and lathering my jaw for a much needed shave. She's the best woman I met in Edinburgh.

I wrote to Peggy reporting the Commission and my leaving Edinburgh. The future life is not a farm, but where God chooses I will go. My feelings could not survive such a return after what farming has done to my family. No, this is my mature deliberation. The question is not into what door of fortune's palace we shall enter, but what entrance she opens to us. This is immediate bread and though poor in comparison with the last eighteen months of my existence, it is luxury compared to my whole preceding life. I was not likely to make an easy gain for I wanted a goal, an ambition, which is a dangerous and unhappy thing. Yet I have got this without mortifying pretension. I count some of the Commissioners as acquaintance and a few as friends.

Tomorrow I take the coach for Glasgow from the White Hart. Retracing Nancy's journey. Perhaps she will be waiting for me, a sole companion like McLehose. I will come back but not to settle. The clatter of the horses is stirring in my blood.

Interleaved letter to Robert Ainslie, stained and crumpled, perhaps inserted by a later hand.

Monday I shall be at the Black Bull in Glasgow to take the morning stage. But tonight I have a whim to write and let you know my movements since leaving Edinburgh. Of course you are not without your own source of news, the fair spy, who receives my occasional reports and tells me in turn of your attentions. 'You must love and cherish Mr Ainslie,' Clarinda instructs me. Beatific Bob. I can feel you smirking at forty miles.

Two weeks have passed since I was at the Bull on the outward leg. My old mentor Captain Brown came to meet me and I poured out the crises of recent months in one great splurge. He was amazed and amused by equal turns, yet it did me good to unlock my sorry luggage and be thoroughly berated as a lily livered epicene for my trouble. Strange how a coach ride and a ribbing begin to change your view of things.

My younger brother Willie joined us, then I fought my way through Paisley and Kilmarnock, pitched against those old familiar foes of mine, the World, the Devil and the Flesh – all three so terrible astride the fields of dissipation. Clarinda's correspondence followed my progress without ever catching me or netting a reply.

For two days I sought refuge at Dunlop House with my former instructress in the ways of polite society. She and all her household made much of the poet's return, though I submitted myself to her chiding on selected episodes of my Edinburgh experience. You, Bob, are sole repository of the whole tale. Beware.

Hearing she was at Tarbolton with the Muirs, I went straight to Jean rather than home to Mauchline. I found

*her with the cargo well laid in, but unfortunately moored
at the mercy of wind and tide. She had been banished
like a martyr, forlorn and destitute, and all for the
good old cause. I reconciled her to her fate, and to her
mother who will attend her lying-in. I towed her into a
convenient harbour, a hired room in Mauchline, where
she may lie snug till unloading. I took her to my arms
– still the same delicious armful – and fucked her till she
rejoiced with joy unspeakable and fullness of glory.*

*But, Bob, I have been prudent and cautious to an
astonishing degree. I swore her privately and solemnly
never to attempt any claim on me as a husband, even
if anybody should persuade her she had such a claim,
which she has not either during my life or after my
death. She did all this like a good girl, so I took the
opportunity of some dry horse litter and gave her such a
thundering scalade as electrified the very marrow of her
bones. What a peacemaker and mediator is a richt guid
weel-willy pintle. He is the pledge and bond of union,
the league and covenant, Aaron's rod and Jacob's staff,
the horn of life and the tree of plenty between man and
woman.*

*Of course I had to report to a certain lady of our
acquaintance and omitted some passages. To compare
Jean with my Clarinda is to set the glimmer of a farthing
taper beside the cloudless meridian sun. Tasteless
insipidity, vulgarity of soul and mercenary fawning. I
have done with her and she with me and so forth.*

*Next it was off to Dumfries to view Patrick Miller's
farm as promised. John Tennant gave it a good report
and advised me to accept the bargain. Old Glen is the
most sensible intelligent farmer in the county, so I was
rocked by his opinion. Now I have two plans of life*

before me. These opinions are private till I return to Edinburgh and meet the Excise.

It was a different story back in Mauchline. Gilbert continues hard-pressed and his landlord, my old friend Gavin Hamilton, tried to persuade me to secure my brother's lease. The language of refusal is the most difficult on earth to me, but I could not undertake this responsibility. He demanded it as if it were his due and was hurt at my refusal. As if I have not a hundred obligations to fulfil! Even so must old acquaintance be forgot.

I wrote to Mrs McLehose on my road home from Cumnock to tell her that the farming scheme may hold, but that you and she are my only confidantes. She writes complaining she has only had one letter from me. Please assure her I wrote from Glasgow, from Kilmarnock, from Mauchline, and then Cumnock.

Also I have religiously observed our sacred Sabbath hour of eight. Mind you, it is apparent that Clarinda has other consolations nearer to hand. My friend, Mr Ainslie, whom I must love and cherish, has called often and alleviated her anxiety. I hear also that she supped again at Kemp's last Friday, so things run on again in their wonted way.

Finally I wrote to Miller to request the lease from Martinmas. The farm is so run-down that all it offers this summer is some grass and tumbled roofs. There will be allowance for a new farmhouse, drainage and fencing. So the poet is not all will-o-the-wisp in this transaction. Perhaps I can still have the Excise too and drive both horses in one harness. Am I the man of business? You would be proud to see my present guiles.

Alas, Robert Muir is a shattered frame waiting to

*meet his Maker. Often when young he gave me a port
in the storm of youthful indiscretion. I could always
depend on friendship and protection at Tarbolton Mill.
An honest man has nothing to fear. If we lie down in the
grave, the whole man a piece of broke machinery, and
moulder with the clods, so be it. At least there is an end
of pain and care, woes and wants. Yet if that part of us
called Mind does survive the apparent destruction of the
man, then there is no truth in old wives' prejudice and
tales. We go to a great unknown Being who has no end
in giving us existence than to make us happy. If that be
atheism then I am King of Siam.*

  *So much, Bob, for philosophy and my news.
Apologies for not writing sooner but apologies for not
writing may be like apologies for not singing – better
than the song. I have fought my way sincerely through
the savage hospitalities of this country and will win back
to Edinburgh early next week. Greet Clarinda with a
kiss.*

  Yours ever, BURNS

Arrived this afternoon. Hied straight to Dowie's then back
to my snug eyrie. Had this delightful room really become
my prison through those leg-bound weeks? Dashed a
note off by urgent messenger to Clarinda, to perch on her
snowy bosom and herald the poet's imminent arrival.

  The town is agog with Deacon Brodie, who has fled
under criminal pursuit. But not for gaming or pimping or
extortion, as one might expect. It transpires the Deacon
had a sideline in armed robbery. By day his legitimate
apprentices would measure locks and doors, hasps and
padlocks, across respectable Edinburgh. By night the

Deacon and his gang went, secret duplicates in hand, to rob and pillage prosperous citizens.

But they overreached themselves by attacking the General Excise Office for Scotland in Chessel's Court – the very place where I pressed my suit for the Commission. Pray God no sortie or surveillance coincided with my visits. They were surprised in the act and fled with only sixteen pounds from the cashier's drawer. Six hundred pounds lay in a secret drawer below – so much for the Deacon's craft! The gang were armed with pistols but withdrew without a shot being fired.

Next, tempted by a government pardon and reward, Brodie's closest turned against his rule. One, Brown, handed himself in for protection, only to receive a prison visit from one of Edinburgh's most prominent citizens – the Deacon! Was murder intended? Whatever, the very next day Brodie fled his native town, followed by a hue and cry across the nation. He has two hundred pounds on his head, and rumour says he has left the country altogether.

Now all spills out in his fleeing wake. Accumulated debts – how could he spend so much? Illicit trades and connections, and horror and delight, three wives with three dependent families – all in God-fearing Reikie's narrow domain. Such entertainment far outruns anything the stage has to offer Edinburgh.

My mind runs over recent months. Is there any trace that could link me to Brodie's dark trades? Thank God I refused his patronage – the double drama of the Deacon must wait another hand. I must steer clear of the Cowgate region, conclude my Edinburgh affairs, and speedily withdraw to Ayrshire. In the eyes of the law I am without reproach.

If he is caught, the Deacon's hanging will be the greatest show the streets have seen since Porteous was strung up. The gibbet is the highest mercy he can plead since short of hanging, drawing and quartering, the affronted pieties can scarcely be appeased. He has squeezed Edinburgh hard in its inmost sanctum, the purse. Unless he can claim the privilege of old status to go beneath his own perfected blade – the Maiden – and see his head tumble cleanly into the basket. Yet some have been known to hang and still survive. The Deacon may gamble on his own demise. Certes, Brodie has broken his reserve with a vengeance to give the poet an unsurpassable tale, which I dare not be the one to tell. His mocking laughter is still ringing in my ears. Bells below, some disturbance. For a moment I am hunted by panic; but it is only some message for the poet, hurriedly delivered... passed upstairs.

Edinburgh is at its end for me. Last words, and farewell. What change a few short days can bring.

Jean gave birth to twins, two lassies, my bonnie little flooers. One dead, the other dying. They'll both be coffined unbaptised before my return. Poor Jean: her second brace. To go full term and see them perish in cauld spring. Twa wee lambs. Nature can be fell cruel.

Creech has finally loosed his grip, one hand at a time. I have half the subscription money but no copyright dues. That must await another siege. Beugo says the old fox may be planning a run of copies behind my back, but he has secretly marked his engravings so that we can detect another printing. I'll expose him if he tries to cheat me, however respectable.

Twin offspring I may have been denied, but I do have a

farm and Instructions for the Excise. The lease for Ellisland is signed, the missives sent. My training for the Customs round begins next month in Ayrshire.

> Searching auld wives' barrels
> Ochon the day
> That clarty barm should stain my laurels
> But what'll ye say!
> These muvin things caad wives an weans
> Wad muve the very herts o stanes.

The night before last, I was handsomely toasted and dined by the Commissioners. Graham of Fintry proved much better than wintry to the bard. Peggy will be pleased to see me settled, though the exertion puts the poet in his early grave. So women wish the best for those they love.

Clarinda and I have parted but I cannot regret our connection. She is the dearest partner of my soul. Wherever we roam, we shall let each other know how we go on. And every week, every fortnight at least, I will send her two or three sheets full of observations, nonsense, news, rhymes and old songs. She will take your place, old faithful friend.

Last night we went out for a stroll up the Lawnmarket onto Castlehill. A fresh clear breeze was blowing from the firth, and the tight green and yellow buds were waiting expectantly to unfurl on all the trees. Our season of concealment was past and over; all was open in the cheering evening light. We wandered back to Potterrow where I had left my presentation gift – two engraved glasses, the tribute of one poet to another.

Fair Empress of the Poet's soul,
And Queen of Poetesses;
Clarinda, take this little boon,
This humble pair of glasses.

She will always remember me by them. Bob and she can toast my memory together. I asked after Jenny, but she seemed to have finished her day's work as usual.

Now that I have a farm, I suppose I should have a wife. In truth I already have the happiness or misery of a much and long-loved fellow creature in my hands. Shall I give her legal title to my body, and farewell rakery! Last time I sat here in the Bull, I had my oldest friend to chaff and chasten, but tonight I have only a book for company.

Even if I do not get polite tattle, modish manners and fashionable dress, I also give boarding-school affectation a wide berth. But I would get the handsomest figure, the sweetest temper, the soundest constitution, and the kindest heart in the country. She mine and I hers, body and soul, in sickness and health, to the close of our days.

When I began this journal, I was at a deal of pain to form a just, impartial estimate of my intellectual and moral powers. Since I went to Edinburgh, I have not added anything to the account. I trust that I am taking every atom of my being back to the shades, the coverts of my early life, the haunts of my remaining years.

EDINBURGH
Fourth Day of November 1788

Deposition
of the Last Wishes of Jenny Clow,
Formerly a Serving Maid

Recorded Verbatim by Robert Ainslie WS
in Niddrie Wynd, Cowgate

I, Jenny Clow, being very sick of a spreading fever, am making my last wishes.

My natural son Robert Burns will go to Mr and Mrs Aitken of Causewayside, who having no children of their own have shown him great kindness. They will care for him and provide. He is nearly three years old.

He is not to be given to his natural father Robert Burns the Poet. Even if he asks.

I thank my mistress Mrs McLehose for her kindness. She did not know of my relations with Burns.

I thank my parents and am sorry for their trouble with me.

The three shillings I got from the Tron Kirk poor box are to go with my child, for him to remember his mother by.

My shawl, spoons and stool are to go to Jessie Haws living in this stair. She and her little girl are also poorly and need money to buy bread.

God have mercy upon us.

This is Jenny Clow

X

Her Mark

Luath Press Limited

committed to publishing well written books worth reading

LUATH PRESS takes its name from Robert Burns, whose little collie Luath (Gael., swift or nimble) tripped up Jean Armour at a wedding and gave him the chance to speak to the woman who was to be his wife and the abiding love of his life. Burns called one of The Twa Dogs Luath after Cuchullin's hunting dog in Ossian's Fingal. Luath Press was established in 1981 in the heart of Burns country, and is now based a few steps up the road from Burns' first lodgings on Edinburgh's Royal Mile. Luath offers you distinctive writing with a hint of unexpected pleasures.
Most bookshops in the UK, the US, Canada, Australia, New Zealand and parts of Europe, either carry our books in stock or can order them for you. To order direct from us, please send a £sterling cheque, postal order, international money order or your credit card details (number, address of cardholder and expiry date) to us at the address below. Please add post and packing as follows: UK – £1.00 per delivery address; overseas surface mail – £2.50 per delivery address; overseas airmail – £3.50 for the first book to each delivery address, plus £1.00 for each additional book by airmail to the same address. If your order is a gift, we will happily enclose your card or message at no extra charge.

Luath Press Limited
543/2 Castlehill
The Royal Mile
Edinburgh EH1 2ND
Scotland
Telephone: 0131 225 4326 (24 hours)
Fax: 0131 225 4324
email: sales@luath. co.uk
Website: www. luath.co.uk